Keeping it in the Family

Pippa Kay

Keeping it in the Family

Acknowledgements

'Stinky Creek' first published in *Malicious Mysteries*,
edited by David Vernon, 2014
'The Fog' first published in *The Common Thread Anthology 2009*,
edited by Jillie Shephard, 2009
'Shadows' first published in *The Common Thread Anthology 2010*,
edited by Jillie Shephard, 2010
'Survivors' first published in *A Tick Tock Heart*, edited by David Vernon, 2014

Keeping it in the Family
ISBN 978 1 76041 545 7
Copyright © Pippa Kay 2018
Cover: four little men in caring hands © zahar2000

First published 2018 by
GINNINDERRA PRESS
PO Box 3461 Port Adelaide 5015
www.ginninderrapress.com.au

Contents

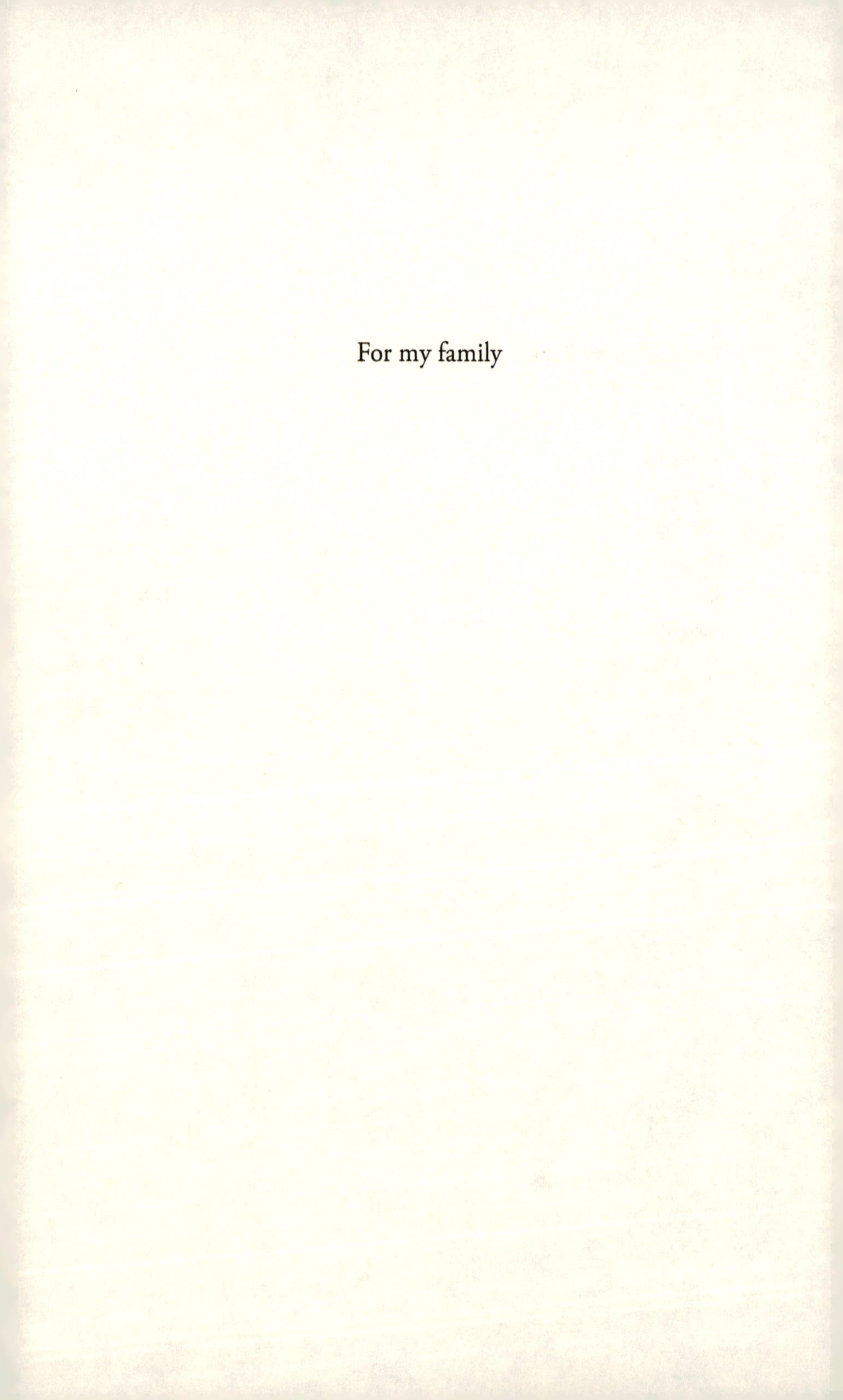

For my family

Keeping it in the Family

'Murder runs in my family,' I warned him, 'and we get away with it.'

He probably thought I was joking, or just didn't hear. More likely he was too busy downing as much beer as possible before six o'clock, closing time. He wasn't a regular. Probably off the ship moored in the dry dock.

'Give us another one, love.' He tossed some pennies onto the bar, which was lathered in beer froth.

I checked the time before pulling another middy and picked up the sopping coins. Four minutes to go. Soon I'd be free of these leering men. They spilled out of their factories at five-thirty, raced up the hill from the dock and the smelter and poured into the hotel a few minutes later, pushing and shoving like pigs in a trough. It was a swill all right.

'Time, gentlemen.' Barry saved my life. 'Drink up, before the coppers come round.' He held the door open for them and gradually the crowd thinned.

Pat, the local constable, was waiting outside. He lived just up the road and had a lock-up behind his house, where he regularly kept drunks until they were sober enough to go back to their families – a popular community service with the women here. Sometimes there were fights, and he hung around the pub until the last of the drinkers had gone. The local workers didn't take kindly to crews from the ships that came into the dock for repairs.

'Everything okay here?' Pat stuck his head in the door checking for stragglers. Seeing the place was empty, he waited for me in the doorway. He usually did this, just in case any ruffians bothered me.

There was no one in sight as I stepped out into the fresh air and crossed the road. I told him I'd be fine and he disappeared inside the pub, where there'd be a middy waiting for him on the bar. He'd drink it and hang around a bit longer while Barry counted the cash from the till.

The pub was at the top of the hill, and when the south-westerly blew, it was shrouded in smoke and ashes from the nearby tin-smelting factory and the dock. This evening it was blowing from the north so it was easier to breathe and I stopped at the top of the cliff to look across the water towards the Harbour Bridge, Cockatoo Island and the city and then down to the dock, a deep gouge carved into the sandstone. I often dreamed of tipping over the edge here – falling but never hitting the bottom. Sometimes I flew, scooped myself up just in time.

When the dock was dry, even the tallest ships were hidden from sight until you peered over the edge. It had been busy during both the wars; passenger and cargo ships were converted to troopships, and then back again after the war. Work at the dock was slowing down now.

I could hear the hum from the pump house. The caisson was closed, plugging the entry to the dock, where a merchant ship had been for the last week; they were pumping water in. It would be a quiet Saturday night, as the crew needed to get back to their ship and prepare for leaving at dawn.

I had my weekly pay in my pocket and a half bottle of claret Barry had given me to take home. He often gave me the dregs, especially on a Saturday evening, because the wine would be no good by Monday. Tomorrow was my day off. Since I'd stopped going to church, I was looking forward to a nice Sunday sleep-in.

Sometimes I felt like a caged animal, with all those men gawking at me, crowding the bar. The smell of them turned my stomach, and their grubby hands repulsed me as they reached out to grab their beer. Some of them would get fresh with me.

I wore a wedding ring, which usually put them off. If they persisted, I told them about my murderous family. Sometimes I told them my husband was waiting for me at home, but I could be caught out with that lie because the locals believed I was war widow, which gave me some respectability in the community. Because my husband had been killed in Tobruk, he was a hero, and I shared some of his glory and gained sympathy. Pity it wasn't true.

I expected I'd end up an old maid, because most of the men I met weren't my kind. I wanted someone with a bit of class. Someone handsome and strong, like Robert Mitchum, or James Stewart.

I smelled his beery breath before I heard him coming up behind me and I jumped away from the edge. The stone fence guarding the cliff edge was low and crumbling.

'Hello,' he said. He was the stranger I'd served at the bar, who'd been trying to get my attention all day, and he was standing between me and the fence. It was tempting. He wouldn't be the first drunk to fall. He staggered, realised how close he was to the edge and stepped away from it. 'You're the barmaid, aren't you? You know how to get away with murder.'

I laughed. 'No, not really.'

I began walking along the ridge, behind the shops to my home. I was living with my gran in a workman's cottage that had been dad's place, and his dad's before him.

He caught up to me. 'P'raps I should see you safely home. There's lots of tramps around…'

'I don't have far to go,' I told him.

'I don't mind.'

I walked briskly, but he kept pace.

'Tell me, how do you get away with murder?' He had a bottle in his pocket, and I could hear coins jingling as he walked.

'I don't know. But it runs in the family. It's a long story,' I said. 'You wouldn't be interested.'

I'd arrived home and leaned against the front fence. He seemed pretty harmless and wasn't bad to look at. He wore a clean white shirt under a grey jacket and trousers and a fedora like Humphrey Bogart's. His shoes were a little scuffed.

'I got the time,' he said. 'Would you like a drink?' He handed the bottle to me, probably expecting me to tip it down my throat like a slut.

Then I realised it was a full bottle of port, a good one at that. 'Where did you get this from?' I asked. 'Did you pinch it?'

'No. Bought it from your boss. God's honour. Gonna sneak it on board. A man's gotta have something to keep out the cold.'

I thought about it for a minute.

'This your place?' he asked. 'You got someone inside waiting for you?'

'Have you got a wife waiting for you somewhere?'

'No. I swear. You got a couple of glasses in there? The night is young,' he said, looking up over the rooftops to the darkening sky. 'And this is a very good drop.'

It would be better than the cheap claret in my pocket, that was certain.

'We might have to share it with my gran,' I said.

Gran was listening to the cricket on the wireless in the living room when we came in, and the room stank of her cigarettes, reminding me of work. She didn't approve of me bringing men home, but it was my house and I could do what I liked. How else was I supposed to meet anyone or have any fun? I introduced him – his name was Les – then we went outside and sat on the cane chairs on the veranda with two glasses and the bottle of port.

He told me he was an engineer on the MV *Bulolo*, which was in the dock for repair work after a fire in the hold. They travel to and from New Guinea, carrying copra back to Australia, but during the war, Les had been in the navy and MV *Bulolo* had been used as a landing ship carrying men and anti-aircraft guns.

It was a balmy spring evening. Jasmine growing over the fence was just in bloom and perfuming the night – a smell I enjoyed for the first couple of weeks, but it soon became cloying and sickly as the weather got hotter. The port was delicious and he refilled my empty glass before topping up his own.

'Your turn,' he said. 'Tell me how to get away with murder. I really want to know.'

'Are you serious?'

'A bit. There's this brute… I think the world would be a better place without him.'

I usually start with the story of my great-grandfather who was a bushranger. People like bushranger stories and it gets them in the mood. 'My great-grandfather shot a man dead in the 1850s. Hid out in a cave for a long time then went north, changed his name and married my great-grandmother who gave birth to my grandfather. No one ever found out.'

'So, how come you know about it if no one ever found out?'

'My great-grandmother spilled the beans after the old man died. The name on his death certificate was different to the name on his birth certificate.'

'Okay, that makes sense, sort of. Who's next?'

'My grandmother.' I pointed inside.

'Who'd she kill?' he whispered.

'I'm not saying.' I swallowed some more port. 'If I told you, I'd have to kill you.'

He laughed. 'No, thank you. So who can you tell me about?'

I shrugged. 'My dad maybe. He's dead now so it doesn't matter.'

'What did he do?'

'Killed my brother. Before I was born, so I never knew my brother.'

'Did he tell you that?'

'No, my mother did. They never married. They just lived together and had me. Everyone thought they were married and that I was an only child. Gran is my mother's mother.' The port loosened my tongue and I told him about life with my parents. 'Dad used to beat Mum and me, and before I was born he'd given my brother a beating and killed him. Little Tommy was only two. After Mum told me, I used to think about it all the time. I was never sure if it was her or Dad who killed Tommy, or if he'd even been killed. Maybe he just got sick and died.

There was a photo of him on Mum's dressing table when I was little. She told me that Dad threatened her and if she ever said anything to the cops he'd tell them she did it, and they'd believe him.'

'Why would they believe him and not her?' Les asked.

'Because Mum was pretty stupid,' I said. 'She hardly ever went to school and couldn't even read a newspaper. I had to do all the shopping because she couldn't add up, and everyone used to take advantage of her. Then she had a nervous breakdown and they locked her up in the lunatic asylum. Maybe it was all the beatings Dad gave her made her so stupid.'

'What about friends and neighbours? Didn't anyone notice the baby wasn't there any more.'

'I don't know. I wasn't even born then, but I think it was after that Dad did some work on the house. He was working at the smelter, and he put in the bathroom and laundry and this veranda.'

'Do you know where the body is?' he asked.

'Mum said they put him in the septic tank.' I held out my glass for some more port. The bottle was half empty.

'Shit.'

I laughed. 'That's right. No one would notice the smell.'

'That's not a bad idea.' He refilled my glass.

'But the brute I want out of the way is a lot bigger than a two-year-old.'

My mouth was dry and I was feeling a bit woozy. I hadn't had any dinner. I should probably get a sandwich or something, but I sipped my port instead.

'I couldn't stand it at home after Mum got put away. It was just Dad and me and I tried to stay out of his way, but I still copped some beatings. Then my gran moved in with us, and after I'd finished at school I got the job at the pub.'

'So your father's dead now.'

'Yes.'

'How did he die?'

'Can't answer that.'

'And your mum?'

'She's still alive, if you can call it any sort of life. Gran and I visit her sometimes and she just sits there, doesn't say anything. I don't think she even knows who we are.' As I took another sip, I splashed some port over my blouse. 'Damn. It'll stain. I'll have to wash it.'

I stood up, a little unsteadily and went in through the laundry to my room. I took off my blouse and pulled on a cardigan, then went back into the laundry, where I filled the tub with some water, while rubbing soap on the spill. It was my best blouse.

He was standing in the doorway, watching me. I hadn't buttoned my cardigan. Then he had his arms around me, turned me to face him, holding my head in both his hands, so tenderly, like I was a precious flower, and he was brushing his lips against my cheeks. I felt myself go weak in his arms, and when our lips met I kissed him like I was dying for it. He wasn't a smoker. His kisses were sweet. I could feel his hands under my unbuttoned cardigan, reaching for my brassiere, fumbling, like someone out of practice.

I pulled myself away from him, turned off the tap and left the blouse to soak. It was quiet in the house, so I figured Gran had gone to bed. I took his hand and led him to my bedroom, closing the door and putting my fingers to my lips, urging him to be quiet.

Our lovemaking was brief and disappointing. I don't know why I expected anything else. After, he slept, as I'd discovered most men do, but I lay awake – thirsty, hungry and headachy. I slipped on my dressing gown and took a powder in the bathroom. He was snoring when I got back. My bed was so narrow and uncomfortable I didn't feel like squeezing in beside him. His wallet was on the dressing table, so I took it out to the kitchen, where I could turn on the light.

There were two five-pound notes, a pound note and a ten-shilling note. I put them back, and then saw a photo. She looked like Marilyn Monroe in a wedding dress. I was furious. With him at first, then with myself. Why were men so rotten? Weren't there any nice ones around?

I thought he was nice for a while, and I'd let him have his way with me. I was just like my mother – a whore and a fool. And like my father, a drunk. And what if I got pregnant? How could I be so stupid? My head was spinning and I had that queasy feeling in my stomach, like I might throw up if I didn't eat something to weigh my tummy down.

I was buttering some bread when I heard him moving about in my bedroom. I stuffed the photo back into his wallet with the notes, and slipped it into my dressing gown pocket.

'I've got to go,' he said, buttoning his shirt and stuffing it into his trousers. 'I've got to get back to the boat. We sail in the morning. Have you seen my wallet?'

'No. Did you look under the bed?' I jumped up and beat him to my room, where I knelt down and pretended to be looking under the bed. 'Here it is,' I called. While I was half under the bed, I fished a note out of the wallet, but it was too dark to see which one. I gave the wallet to him, and continued making my sandwich.

He didn't even say thank you, but opened his wallet and pulled out the notes.

I began chewing on the bread.

'I thought I had more than this…' he said.

I shrugged. 'Would you like a sandwich?' I offered, picking up a sharp knife and sawing into the loaf.

'Please.' He sat down at the table and watched me make him a honey sandwich, like I was his servant.

'When will I see you again?' I asked, unable now to stop the tears. They were angry tears, though, not sad tears.

Gran came into the kitchen, looking like an old witch in her raggedy nightgown, with her grey hair all frizzed up around her face, and no teeth in her mouth.

'So you're still here,' Gran mumbled on her way through to the bathroom. She slammed the door.

'I'll be back in a couple of months,' he whispered to me. 'I'll see you then. Promise.'

'S'pose you have to go back to your wife,' I said, nearly choking on a lump of crust caught in my throat.

'I'm not married.'

'Then who's the girl in the photo?' I asked.

'You *did* have my wallet! You *did* take my money?' This time he didn't whisper.

The toilet flushed and Gran emerged from the bathroom. 'Everything all right, dear?' she asked, standing in the doorway with her arms crossed over her chest. 'I think it's time you left, young man.' She wasn't going to move. She could be pretty scary for an old lady.

Les picked up his coat and went out through the lounge room and front door, and I thought that would be the last time I ever saw him.

*

There was half a bottle of port and a fedora on the veranda. I brought them both inside then decided to run a bath. Impatient with the chip heater, I sat in lukewarm water for a few minutes, sobbing and trying to cleanse myself of that man.

I was drying off in the bedroom, considering another glass of port, to help me sleep, when I heard tapping on the window. I shrugged into my dressing gown and pulled up the blind.

It was Les. I opened the window. 'What do you want?' I asked.

'I left my hat here.'

I threw it out the window.

'I didn't want to say goodbye like that,' he said, not bothering to pick up his precious hat. 'I *will* be back. Will you write to me, care of MV *Bulolo*?'

I sat on my bed, blew my nose and dried my eyes with a hanky, while he climbed in through the window.

'Your gran looks pretty frightening,' he said, sitting down on the bed beside me.

'You better believe it,' I said.

'Is it true she murdered someone?'

'Yes.'

'Who?'

'My father.'

'And did she dump his body in the septic tank?'

'No.'

'Where?'

'Off the cliff.'

'Nah, I don't believe that. She's pretty fierce-looking, but she doesn't look strong enough to drag a grown man…'

'We used the wheelbarrow.'

'We? You mean, you and your gran? Is that true?'

'It was in the papers.' I got up and showed him the newspaper cutting I kept in my top drawer. *Body found on dry dock.*

'Shit.' He read the story. 'They thought he was drunk and slipped.'

I nodded. 'Dad was a bad drunk, but he wasn't always drunk, if you know what I mean. He'd get a job, work hard, make good money, and then something would just go snap and he'd go on a drinking binge. Everyone round here knew that. And when he was drunk he was violent. Gran and I used to hide from him. He came home one day, broke down my door and started hitting me. Gran came into the room and hit him over the head with a full bottle of beer, and he just crumpled. There was a lot of blood, but we didn't think he was dead. Just thought he was out to the world. She said it was a waste of good beer. We opened another one to celebrate. Wasn't until I tried to drag him out of my room…'

I looked at him, and realised I'd just blurted out the big secret, and I didn't know anything about this guy, apart from the fact that he was married. 'That's got you worried now, hasn't it?' I laughed. 'Pity it's not true.'

'So how did he die?'

'Just like it said in the newspaper. He got drunk and slipped over the edge.'

He thought about it for a minute, and I could tell from his expression that he wasn't sure what to believe.

'How about you get dressed and walk with me for a bit?' he asked. 'So we can say goodbye properly. I don't want to leave you but I really must.'

*

He was quiet as we walked. I felt quite sober now. More in control.

I had a lot of unanswered questions. 'What's her name?' I asked, when we stopped at the cliff edge.

He stood well back. 'Laura.'

'And where is she? Port Moresby? Brisbane? One of the islands?'

'Brisbane.'

'Are you going to tell her about me?'

'I don't know.'

'What'll happen if I get pregnant?'

'I don't know. I – I'll look after you, I promise.'

'Give me your wallet. Let me have another look at her.'

'No.'

'Why not? You don't trust me, do you?'

'Okay. Here you are.' He pulled out his wallet and gave me her photo.

There wasn't much point, because it was very dark and I could hardly see anything. But I held on to it and pretended to be studying it as I walked closer to the edge.

'Let's not be silly,' he said. 'Why don't you just come here and give me a kiss. I've got to go.'

'No, you come here and I'll give you a kiss.'

He hesitated, moved closer, held me in his arms and bent to kiss me. I flung the photo of his wife over the edge. That'll teach him. He released me to catch her. I pushed him. Down he went, screaming. I heard the splash. The dock was almost full of water now.

17

It had happened so fast. Did anyone see? Unless someone was hiding in the shadows, I seemed to be alone.

His scream echoed in my brain. Someone must have heard that. I had to think. Lights flicked on behind me in the pub. I ran down the lane behind the shops, where it was darkest. I tripped on a tree root and fell, grazed my knee. Picked myself up and felt my way along the back fences to the end of the lane. Then it was only a short way to my home and I kept to the shadows cast by trees. I dared not look back. Down the side of my house to my open bedroom window. I climbed in.

*

Sometimes I wake up and can't remember where I am or what happened the night before, especially after I've been drinking. Sunday was one of those days. My mouth felt dry and my head was aching. I could hear Gran in the kitchen and smell the toast she was burning. On my dressing table there was a bottle of port and some loose change.

I rolled over in bed and my knee stung.

My bedroom window was wide open. Was it open like that before I went to bed? Then I flung back the bedclothes and saw blood on the sheets, and that reminded me of Dad, though there was much more blood the night Gran killed him. I was a bit slow this morning but I soon realised this was my blood and it had come from my knee, which was badly grazed.

How did I do that? I remembered a dream I'd had, where I was stumbling around in the dark. Someone was screaming. I was running away. Was someone chasing me?

I was like my dad, a bad drunk. I have nightmares too. If I think about them too much, I start to believe they really happened. I'm scared one day I'll turn into my mother and be locked up in the lunatic asylum. She used to carry on with all this rubbish, about Dad killing my brother, and I was never sure if it was true or something she'd dreamt up.

Someone was knocking on the front door, and that reminded me of something else – someone knocking on my window.

I got up and dressed slowly. Gran would open the door. She'd take care of whatever the person wants. It's Sunday. My day off. I can't be bothered.

'Who was that?' I asked, when I was dressed and ready for some breakfast.

'Just Pat, doing the rounds. There was an accident last night. Some drunk did a high dive into the dock and drowned. What did you say that young man's name was last night? Des, wasn't it?'

It was coming back to me. I cut a thick slice from the loaf of bread and lit the grill on the Kooka. 'Something like that,' I said, remembering the man at the hotel who was trying to chat me up. Les, not Des.

'I didn't say anything to Pat about your visitor. It would just make things complicated, wouldn't it.'

'You sent him packing.' I remembered.

My toast was ready. I took it out, spread it with butter and poured some tea from the pot Gran had made.

Usually I don't like to think about the past. I've no good memories. Instead I daydream about how things might be one day. Maybe I'll meet someone nice, maybe I'll have a baby. But who will it be like? Me? My mum? My dad? My gran? Or Les?

If I get pregnant, I'll have to get rid of it. I couldn't bring a kid into my family.

I thought about Les, his plunge into the dark, the way he screamed. When I threw that photo and he tried to catch it, I knew he loved her more than me, more than his life was worth. But he was cheating on her. And I did warn him. He deserved to die.

I was scared last night, and maybe a little sorry, but not now. Murder runs in our family and I can't be blamed for what happens.

Hear No Evil

When he was five, Peter woke up one morning with something strange on the pillow beside his head. It was a very long ear. He felt it with his hand, like a rabbit's ear; and there was another one on the other side of his head.

Peter ran into his mummy's and daddy's room, to tell them about his new ears. They were asleep. He could tell that Mummy was dreaming about an earthquake – it was pretty scary, and Peter was glad he didn't have dreams like that. Daddy was dreaming about the lady next door, and it seemed to be a nice dream.

He tugged them out of their dreams. 'Look, Mummy, I've got ears!'

'Of course you've got ears,' said Mummy, who was relieved to be woken.

'They're big!' Peter said. 'Can't you see them?'

'They look pretty normal to me.' She stroked his head, and he could feel her hand on his hair and scalp, not on his ears.

Later, looking at his face in the mirror, he realised his new big ears were invisible, which explained why no one could see them.

It was Easter and after breakfast he and his brother Allen had an Easter egg hunt. Peter got all the eggs and Allen thought it wasn't fair.

His mother assumed Peter had been watching when she and Daddy hid them last night. Allen didn't believe in the Easter bunny anyway.

'D'you think Santa isn't true either?' Peter asked, with his mouth full of chocolate, and handing one of the eggs to his big brother.

There was a whoosh of thoughts then: Mummy didn't want Allen to say anything; Daddy thought Peter should know the truth by now; Allen was only interested in scoring more Easter eggs from his little brother, and was trying to work out the best way.

Then Peter realised he was listening in on everyone's thoughts. He put his hands over his ears, dropping all the eggs while Allen scooped them up, thinking this was too easy, while his mother wondered if she should take him to the doctor and his father wasn't paying any attention to what was happening inside the house because he could see the lady next door on her veranda, and she was still in her nightdress.

It was a terrible day. Peter spent most of it in his room, away from people, because it was just so confusing. His big ears weren't a gift, they were a curse. Who wanted to know what everyone else was thinking?

At school, Peter learned many ways to cope with the intrusion of other people's thoughts. One of them was tapping – tapping on his school desk, tapping on the dining room table, tapping on the back of the seat in front of him on the train; he created complicated rhythms that demanded concentration.

People were annoyed by the tapping, especially grown-ups. They thought he only did it when he was bored, so they challenged him with new and interesting activities. He learned to concentrate, to focus his thoughts on what he was doing, one thing at a time, and apart from when he was tapping, he was a quiet child. Other children thought he was a bit strange, and some adults, such as his doctor and a child psychologist, thought he might be autistic or schizophrenic.

He learned not to talk about his ears and hearing people's thoughts, fearing they'd put him on medication or lock him up in some sort of institution – or both. His hair grew thick on his scalp, through his ears, which remained invisible. Only he could feel them.

*

Not surprisingly, Peter did well at school. However, it was his skill at concentration and his ability to tune out all distractions that gave him the edge; not mind-reading. Sitting in an exam room with a hundred other students was like trying to do a multiple-choice exam with a hundred possible answers. Often, when there were complaints about him tapping, the examiners would put him in a room on his own.

His parents had ambitious plans for him – engineering, medicine or politics. It was possible, they thought, that he might become prime minister. Peter wasn't sure how he was going to break it to his parents, but what he really wanted to do was be a drummer in a band.

When he was fifteen, his father sat him down for one of those father-son talks about sexual responsibility and respect for the opposite sex. What a hypocrite, thought Peter, who knew about his father's affair with gorgeous Linda next door.

'What about you and Linda then?' asked Peter. 'Mum'd be very upset if she knew.'

His father reddened. 'We're just good friends, good neighbours.'

Peter tapped out a complicated rhythm to try and block the jumble of thoughts and emotions from his father, who took this tapping to be a sign of his son's indifference and put his hands on Peter's wrists to stop him, wondering if there was something he could do to guarantee Peter's silence on the matter; such as a bribe.

'You know what I really want, Dad,' Peter said at last. 'I'd like a drum kit, a proper one, not a toy like those bongos you bought me when I was twelve. And I'd like to be a drummer in a band.'

'Well, why not,' said his father, smiling, thinking this won't last, it'll be another teenage fad, and he'll outgrow it eventually. 'Let's go and have a look at drum kits on the weekend. And…you won't say anything to your mother, will you?'

'Not about Linda, Dad, but I'm sure she's going to know about the drum kit when I get it.'

*

When he was sixteen, Peter formed a band called the Know It Alls with guys from school. Most of their gigs were at school dances for little or no payment. The Know It Alls broke up when they finished school.

He went to uni and studied political science because his parents still dreamed of him becoming prime minister.

He kept tapping on desks and tables, walked around with earbuds playing music most of the time and practised drumming at home, much to his parents' annoyance. He did the occasional gig with pub bands and earned a little money. By his second year at uni, his reputation had grown and he was working most weekends, and he could afford to move into a flat with other musicians.

When his parents helped him move, he couldn't block out their mishmash of emotions. They looked forward to the peace and quiet that they'd now have at home, and worried that his studies might suffer. His father bought him an old station wagon so he could transport his drum kit around from gig to gig, while his mother feared he'd have a car accident. Again, his brother thought it wasn't fair, that Peter was the favourite son; and he was right.

He quit uni in his third year, having joined the Movers and Shakers when their drummer went into rehab, just before they were about to tour the major cities in Australia and New Zealand. Their latest single, 'Wishin'', was topping the charts. This was big-time. The concerts attracted thousands of fans and Peter did long solos to thunderous applause.

Peter hadn't had much time for romance. In fact, he found talking to girls very confronting and confusing. They were usually older, and often drunk, especially in the pub-band days. When the music stopped and he heard their thoughts, which seemed so shallow, he quickly lost interest. He lived up to the popularly held belief that drummers were either stupid or strange because, despite his success, he was very shy and always sober. Alcohol really messed with his brain, and he'd never tried drugs.

After their last concert in Adelaide, while the band and crew got boozed, Peter walked through Rundle Mall with his ear buds firmly lodged in his ears. He realised he was lonely and cursed his big ears. Suddenly he heard a voice that didn't belong on that track. Someone was singing along, and it was such a sweet, sweet voice. He pulled the earbuds out and looked around, hearing her thoughts immediately.

She knew he was hearing them because she was hearing his.

It had never occurred to him that there might be others in the world like him. And here she was, now, standing in front of him, a petite blonde with the cutest rabbit ears.

They stared at each other for a few minutes until she put her hands over them to block out his thoughts. 'Stop it,' she said aloud. 'I'm getting confused.'

'I can't stop thinking.'

'Nor can I.'

So he kissed her and gave her something to think about that they could both enjoy.

Paloma

1

We'd won the auction, and a week after the contract and money business was finished, we took a few things over there. I wandered around the backyard feeling very pleased with myself. It just seemed right somehow, that I might end my days where I'd begun them – in this house, with this backyard.

I wasn't under any illusions. It needed a lot of work. The previous owner, who had probably bought the house from my parents, had done very little to it except to bring the bathroom, with a flushing toilet, indoors. It was tiny: two-and-a-half bedrooms, the half-bedroom being an enclosed veranda. Well, we were wanting to downsize.

The paling fence between our place and what used to be Paloma's was falling down, crushed, it seemed, by a monstrous passionfruit vine. It looked very different on this side of the yard. We used to grow chokos.

My wife, Barbara, found me in the yard. I was standing under the jacaranda on a carpet of purple flowers, remembering my mother watering it when it was just a precious seedling.

'There's someone wants to see you,' she said. 'Out the front.'

'Who?'

'I don't know. But she asked me if we were the new owners and if your name was John Higgins.'

I was curious.

'Remember me?' she asked when I greeted her at the front door. 'You told me you'd teach me how to fly.'

'Paloma!' I wrapped my arms around her and gave her a hug. 'What the… Do you…? You don't still live next door, do you?'

'No.'

I could just see the scar from her lip surgery and hear that slight mumble in her speech. If you'd just met her, though, you'd never know she was born with a cleft palate.

'Paloma, this is my wife, Barbara.'

They shook hands. A more formal greeting. And I was beginning to wonder if I should have greeted her so enthusiastically.

'Come on in.' I opened the door for her. 'Sorry, we haven't actually moved in yet, but we've got a couple of boxes to sit on and I can make us a cuppa.'

She struggled up the steps with her walking cane in one hand and the other pulling on the banister. Her bad leg seemed much more withered now. 'You look well,' she said.

I couldn't say the same for her, and she saved me the trouble.

'I came to the auction and saw you bidding, and I wondered if it was really you.' Then she turned to Barbara. 'Does he still tell whopping great lies?' she asked.

Barbara laughed. 'Well, he is a little prone to exaggeration.'

I thought I'd better explain. 'Paloma used to live next door, and when I first met her, she'd just come out of hospital. She was on crutches.' Then I wondered if she would resent me telling my wife this, and looked to Paloma to see how she reacted.

'Actually, he told me he could fly,' she said, smiling. 'And I believed him. He said he could only fly at night when the moon was full, and that he'd show me how to do it one night.'

Barbara laughed. 'Just like Peter Pan. That'd be right. He's never grown up.'

I felt myself blushing and got busy unpacking the kettle, some mugs and tea bags. 'I hope you don't have milk,' I said.

'Black is fine.' She seated herself on a box which I hoped would hold her weight, because she was now quite a large woman.

Barbara sat opposite her on another box. 'Darling,' she said, 'we must bring a couple of chairs.' Then turning to Paloma, 'We're a bit rough and ready, I'm afraid. Haven't sold the other house yet, and we're trying to work out what to do with this place. John has very fond memories and he's a bit sentimental about things, so he's reluctant to pull it down, but really, it's a demolition job. Don't you agree?'

They watched in silence as I poured water onto the tea bags, and handed mugs to both women.

'I'm sure Paloma's not interested in our plans,' I said. 'Where are you living now?'

'Not far away, actually. I've got a unit near the shopping centre. It's quite comfortable and all I need.' She sipped her tea, watching me over the lip of her cup. 'Do you have a family?'

'Yes,' Barbara answered, and went on to tell her about our two sons and four grandchildren, all living interstate now.

'I never married,' said Paloma. 'It's just me and Toby, now.'

'Toby?'

'He's a miniature foxy – brown spots, floppy ears. The tenants in the other units don't mind him, because he doesn't make much noise and I'm on the ground floor with a little courtyard. He's just had his sixteenth birthday.'

'Did you give him a party?' I was joking but she took it seriously.

'Of course. All the children in the units came and we had a cake and party hats. They all thought it was fun. But I couldn't have any chocolate crackles because you know chocolate isn't good for dogs.' She dug into her handbag and produced a photo which she showed us of a small dog wearing a tiny paper hat sitting beside a blue cake with sixteen lit candles.

I wasn't going to ask if he blew the candles out by himself. I'm well aware that elderly ladies with miniature dogs can talk endlessly about them, even more than real parents with real children.

Barbara, sensing my impatience, changed the subject. 'I'm curious to know more about John when he lived here,' she said. 'How long did he keep up this story about being able to fly?'

'Oh, years! I was about five, I think, when we moved here and I have to confess I was a little bit in love with your husband. I didn't want it not to be true, you see, like Santa Claus and the tooth fairy.' She sipped her tea and frowned. 'I had a lot of problems. I had polio when I was a baby, and this leg just didn't grow properly, and I had a harelip, and operations on that, and so I was late starting school. I was seven. Two years older than most children. And then the other children were horrible to me. Only John wasn't.'

Both women were grinning at me, like I was some sort of hero. Tears welled in Paloma's eyes – mint-green, unusual but very familiar to me, a jolt from my past, even in her older face. Now perhaps more like her father's eyes, which were the same colour.

'What about your parents?' I asked. 'Are they still alive?'

'No, I'm an orphan now. And you?'

'We've both lost our parents too.'

'I lived next door most of my life really,' she explained. 'After my parents died, I sold the house and bought my little unit – that must be fifteen years ago now. Toby had just had his first birthday.'

'Your old place has had some work done on it.' I commented, trying to steer the conversation away from Toby or anything too emotional.

'Yes, it's a pity. But the whole area has undergone a lot of change – very upmarket nowadays. Remember the outdoor dunnies and the dunny man? And the houses were smaller and we all grew vegies.'

I drank my tea quickly, and began to wish she'd hurry up and finish hers. I looked at my watch. The afternoon was getting away from us, and I'd wanted to take up some of the lino in the kitchen to see what the floorboards were like.

She took the hint, drained her cup and stood. 'Well, I mustn't keep you. You've obviously got things to do.'

I took her cup.

'You must leave us your phone number,' said Barbara, 'and come for dinner or a barbecue when we're a bit more settled.'

Barbara found a scrap of paper in the kitchen and they swapped phone numbers and email addresses. After she'd gone, Barbara turned on me. 'I can't believe how rude you were. That poor woman. Standing there, looking at your watch, like you've got something important to do.'

'Well, I have!' I crouched down on the kitchen floor and lifted a corner of the cracked lino. 'See, I told you the floor would be good. We can polish this up – it'll look great.'

'No, we won't! We're calling in the bulldozers.'

Barbara won the argument. A few days after the bulldozers began destroying my childhood home, we received an email from Paloma, inviting us to lunch at her place. We had some interested buyers for our current home but it was still unsold so we were dipping into our savings.

Armed with a sad bunch of red roses and a box of chocolates, I knocked on the front door of the address she'd given us. I could hear a dog yapping. It stopped suddenly as the door opened. Paloma held the little beast in her arms.

We squeezed past her, the hall being narrow, one wall occupied by a cluttered antique hallstand. It was laden with books, ornaments, a raincoat, assorted scarves and a huge sun hat, which I managed to bump from its hook and catch with the roses.

'Sorry,' I said, as petals fluttered to the floor.

'Oh, how lovely,' said Paloma, putting Toby down before rescuing her hat and the roses. The dog promptly took a flying leap for my trouser cuffs and began to hump my leg as I limped after Barbara and Paloma into the living room.

It was a gloomy room, overcrowded with large pieces of furniture and smelling of dog. The curtains were closed and it felt claustrophobic.

Paloma finally noticed Toby on my leg. 'Toby! Stop that.' She picked him up again. 'He's not used to strangers. You're not a teenager any more, you naughty boy.'

For a flash, I thought she was talking to me, but she snuggled her face into Toby's and gave him a kiss.

I shuddered.

'Please, sit down.' She gestured to the overstuffed lounge suite that took up most of the floor space.

I remembered it from her parent's house.

'What can I get you?' asked Paloma. 'Beer, wine?'

'A glass of water would be lovely,' I said, hoping Barbara would follow my lead.

I wanted to get this over with as quickly as possible, but Barbara gave me her saccharine smile, knowing exactly how I was feeling, and requested a glass of white wine.

Paloma either misheard me or ignored me and placed three glasses of white wine on the coffee table in front of us. Toby jumped up on the lounge and sat between us while Paloma disappeared into the kitchen again. Barbara stroked him and he put his head on her thigh.

Paloma came back into the room with a tray-load of gold-rimmed floral dishes full of olives, nuts and crackers. 'Oh, just look at you. Look at those great big puppy-dog eyes.' Again, I thought she was talking to me – I'm often accused of having great big puppy-dog eyes, especially when I want something. 'Toby only does that to people he trusts. Is the wine cold enough?'

I took a sip and nodded. Barbara added that it was very nice.

Paloma urged us to eat up, said she had a lamb roast in the oven, something about remembering I always liked roast lamb and then something about Tom Cruise that I didn't understand but drew a polite laugh from Barbara.

At last lunch was ready and we moved to one end of the dining table, the other end being against the wall, and on that wall was a framed print of Picasso's *Child with Dove*. It used to be in Paloma's childhood room.

'Remember this table?' Paloma asked me.

'Yes, we used to play under it,' I explained to Barbara, trying to shake Toby off my leg as I sat down.

'It extends and can seat twelve, but of course there isn't room for that here.' She served the meat and vegetables. 'Help yourselves to gravy.'

As I reached for the pepper and salt, I trod on Toby's tail and he yelped.

Paloma ducked her head and shoulders under the table and dragged Toby away from me. 'Oh, you are such a naughty boy today,' she said, feeding the dog with meat on her fork. 'Excuse me, I'll just pop Toby in my bedroom. He's being a bit of a nuisance, isn't he?'

She disappeared into another room, where she must have turned on the television, because I could hear those squeaky American voices from children's television shows.

She plonked herself down in her chair again. 'Luckily *Dora the Explorer*'s on,' she said, finishing the mouthful of meat on her fork. 'His favourite show.'

I nodded, catching a smirk from Barbara, who was having trouble keeping a straight face.

'Now, tell me what you're planning to build on your parent's land,' Paloma asked, and I let Barbara explain her plans because, after all, I've had very little to do with it. She'd been spending so much time with her young architect, I'd accused her of having an affair. I was joking but she didn't seem to find it funny.

Meanwhile, I ate in silence, remembering a time in my teens when Paloma and I hid under the dining table while her parents were out. She was the first girl I'd ever kissed. She'd told me she was frightened that boys wouldn't want to kiss her because of her lip. I was more than happy to oblige and, even as a novice girl-kisser, I'd found it very nice. She'd noticed my erection, and giggled as she stroked it through my jeans, until we heard her parents come in the front door. We'd scrambled out and pretended to be working on homework when they entered the dining room. I'd winked at her. She'd given me her crooked grin. I thought I was in love. But I was ashamed of myself too. I was like her big brother, and kissing her, getting an erection, felt incestuous, and there was something perverse about loving a girl with a crooked mouth and a withered leg. My parents would be horrified.

Barbara and I laughed as we drove home. Everyone used to laugh at Paloma. Now my wife was making fun of her too, and I felt uncomfortable about it.

Then Barbara changed her tune. 'You know, I feel very sorry for Paloma. And I think you could have been a bit more sympathetic. The poor dear was trying so hard.' She giggled again. 'It was funny, though, wasn't it?'

'It was funny and sad, I guess,' I said. 'She's changed a lot. When we were young, she was quite a plucky little kid – you know, she never felt sorry for herself or anything, and some of the kids at school were cruel.'

'I can imagine.'

'That's why I made up the thing about flying. We used to talk about it a lot. It seemed to me that it'd be good for her to have something to hold on to, a dream, even if it was impossible.'

'That was very mature of you,' she said.

'I was a lot older than her in many ways. I mean, she was only a few months younger than me really, but at school she was two years behind me, because of polio and the lip and lots of things really. Her father was in the army before they moved next door and they'd moved from place to place.'

'You look a lot younger than her now.'

'So do you.'

'I should hope so. She must have let herself go.'

Barbara was very critical of people who *let themselves go* and was constantly watching what we ate and making sure we got plenty of exercise. She claimed it was more important now that we'd both retired, because *health is everything*. Sometimes she overdid things, though, was borderline obsessive. There were times when I would have enjoyed that extra glass of wine.

I had to agree with her concerning Paloma. 'Of course, anyone might let themselves go if they had to endure what Paloma suffered.'

'Was she…' Barbara hesitated, 'abused?'

'No, I don't think so. Not by her parents or teachers but bullied by the children at school. They could be so cruel.'

At last we were in our street.

Barbara was rummaging in the glovebox for the remote for the gate. 'I suppose it would have been tough in those days, before political correctness,' she said with her usual scoffing tone, pushing the remote button with some force. She hated political correctness.

I wanted to defend Paloma. Instead, I drove into our garage.

*

I didn't sleep again that night. I'd been tossing and turning most nights worrying about the house not selling and the money we were spending. Barbara seemed quite happy to hire an architect and contractors to do this and do that, but we couldn't afford it. Soon we'd have to get a loan. At our age!

I drifted off eventually and dreamed about crows – lined up on the fence between Paloma's and our place. Then they swarmed, like bees. It was mayhem. Feathers everywhere. I couldn't breathe. I woke up coughing, choking on feathers.

'What's the matter?' Barbara was only half awake, but it was enough to be annoyed with me. 'Go get yourself a glass of water.'

I went into the kitchen, drank some water, then sat down at the dining table and turned on my computer to Google *a collective word for crows*. A murder of crows. I shuddered and added a nip of Scotch to my water.

This was a recurring dream, which usually had me coughing and spluttering in the night. Sometimes I was choking on pollen, sometimes it was moths or butterflies. My doctor thought I might have sleep apnoea or reflux.

Then I remembered Paloma's parents building that pigeon loft in their backyard, along the fence between our houses, where the passionfruit vine is now. The choko vine had grown over the fence and the loft.

I'd just started high school; Paloma was still in primary school.

At twelve, she was much taller than her ten- and eleven-year-old classmates, and much taller than me. I'd noticed she was growing breasts and was curious to get a glimpse of them. I spent a lot of time at my bedroom window looking into her house and her backyard, but the loft put a stop to that, because it completely blocked my view. I believed her parents had built it there to stop my spying on Paloma.

Barbara came into the dining room. It was seven o'clock in the morning. The sun was shining and I'd just downed the dregs of my whisky. She'd caught me. Guilty.

That weekend, we met the architect at the site. It was no longer my old home. We walked through the rubble, paced out the new living room, the kitchen, bathrooms (three!) and bedrooms (four).

'I thought we were supposed to be downsizing!' I said. 'This place is going to be even bigger than our current home.'

'Not really,' said our architect. 'There's no wasted space. We can fit more into a home that's well designed. It'll all be on one level and designed for climate.' He waved a floor plan at me, but I wasn't wearing my glasses.

'John is very worried about the cost,' Barbara explained. 'But I'm sure we'll sell our old house soon.'

'And then where will we live?' I said.

Barbara rubbed my back, her signal for me to calm down.

Leaving them to it, I made my way to the backyard, where there were so many memories. I got down on my hands and knees to explore under the vine, to see if any of the fence was worth preserving, and picked some ripe passionfruit, stuffing them into all my pockets, feeling like a thief on my own land.

We still hadn't met our new neighbours, and I'd have to talk to them about this fence. No time like the present, I thought. I stepped over the remains of the fence and walked to their front door.

A young woman answered the doorbell. From somewhere in the house I could hear the voices of an adult male and a small child.

I explained who I was and offered her some passionfruit.

'Oh, thanks, but sorry, we don't like them. Too many seeds.' She invited me into their house.

Sunlight streamed into their kitchen and family room, which looked out onto the fence and vine. I could smell freshly brewed coffee.

'Would you like a cup?' offered her husband. 'I'll make it.'

We wandered over to the fence and vine with our cappuccinos – they had a coffee machine.

'I used to live next door when I was young,' I told them.

'Really! That's amazing.'

'There was a pigeon loft where the vine is. And a fig tree in the middle of your yard with a swing. You've done a lot of work to this place. The garden looks…well, quite different. It's very nice.' I could see Barbara and the architect on the other side of the fence and waved to them.

'We're planning to put a pool in,' the woman said. 'Here.' She pointed to where the tree used to be. 'So we'll have to discuss all that with you, but for the moment, all I really want is a fence that'll keep a small child in and intruders out.'

I nodded. 'I was thinking of building the fence myself. Would you be happy with a paling fence? I've done it before. All you'll need to worry about is half the cost of materials.'

'That sounds brilliant,' said her husband. 'We can paint it if you like.'

Barbara and our architect came over and introductions were made. Our architect gave them his card and told them to ring him if they had any problems or issues; we shook hands and I stepped back over the fence to our side.

'Were they homing pigeons?' the woman asked.

'Yes, they were.'

I remembered my dream. Pigeons, of course. Paloma, named after the song, 'La Paloma', the little dove. Dove, pigeon, same thing.

I took a small shovel and mattock from the boot of our car and returned to the passionfruit vine. Since we were paying for the removal of the building rubbish, I could at least add some old fence posts. While Barbara was chatting to the architect, I thought I'd make a start. Some physical work might help me sleep.

I remembered those pigeons. Paloma's father had been involved in some sort of carrier pigeon espionage during the war. There were lots of stories about it. I'd believed them then but now they seem a bit far-fetched. Like 007 goes to New Guinea, a wild, mountainous place full of savages, and heroic tales of getting troops across enemy lines.

Every morning, the pigeons were set free. There'd be a whoosh of wings as they escaped and swirled around our house like a whirlwind, then came to rest on our fence, on the dunny roof, on the rotary clothes line or in the jacaranda tree, which was a couple of metres high then. And there'd be bird shit all over our grass. Mum never left clothes on the line overnight. Even now, whenever I hear the sound of pigeons cooing, or that rush of wings when a flock of birds take off, I break out in a cold sweat. Of course, Paloma loved it. She was usually the one to set them free. She wanted to fly like them.

And I wanted to teach her to fly.

Sometimes I'd push her on the swing, even though she was quite capable of pushing herself. She'd go very high and threaten to jump off, to fly over the roof. Sometimes she'd let go the ropes, teasing me, but she never flew.

Her mother would be watching from the kitchen window and she'd come out screaming at me, 'Are you trying to kill her?' even when I wasn't doing the pushing.

I felt a shadow over me and straightened up to see Barbara blocking the sun.

'What on earth are you doing?' she asked.

'I thought I'd try and save some money by building the fence myself.'

'That's okay, but you don't have to do that. We can get the bulldozer to rip down the fence.'

'Actually, I was hoping to save the passionfruit vine.'

She shook her head and looked at me as if I were crazy. 'We can plant another one when the new fence is built, if you like.'

*

After demolishing my parents' home, the bulldozers tore down the jacaranda tree, the fence and passionfruit vine. Then they began excavating for the underground two-car garage. Our old backyard looked like a moonscape.

I had a load of timber delivered for the fence, and measured up, wanting to get the fence done quickly to keep our neighbours happy.

Their child watched and asked endless questions. 'Why are you digging a hole?' 'Can I help?' 'What's that for?' and I tried to explain about needing a strong post, about how concrete set, and what a string-line was for. It was a challenge.

At last, his mother called him inside.

Perhaps it was better to demolish the old house, I decided. Since buying the property, I was being haunted by memories, not all of them good.

2

On the night of my eighteenth birthday, we had a party in our backyard. We'd cleaned the bird shit off everything, Dad cooked sausages and lamb chops and Mum made a potato salad and buttered lots of bread. I put my portable turntable on an old table, and my record collection, which consisted of three LPs: the Beatles, the Rolling Stones and the Doors. Some of the guys would bring more music, and we'd dance under the Hill's Hoist clothes line. I hoped the wind wouldn't blow from the south, as that was where the dunny was.

Mum had made a very diluted punch – mostly orange juice, with cut-up lemon wedges, and a bottle of Porphyry Pearl to give it some fizz. Of course, I complained about that. We should have some beer. At eighteen I'd be at the legal age for drinking alcohol, and I'd already had the occasional beer with Dad. However, Mum was old-fashioned, and had an overgrown sense of responsibility. I was one of the oldest in my group of friends, and most of the girls we'd invited were a couple of years younger.

I'm not proud of the young man I was then, and meeting Paloma reminded me of what an arrogant and selfish prick I'd been.

I'd finished school and, with good marks, enrolled in civil engineering – the first in my family to go to university, as my parents constantly reminded me. None of my schoolmates were going to uni, and I thought I was better than them. Most had labouring jobs. None of the girls who came to my party had stayed on for the leaving certificate; they were working as shop assistants or learning hairdressing. Paloma was going to business college studying typing and shorthand.

Uni hadn't started yet, but when it did, I was sure I'd find a better class of friend. Meanwhile, I just had to endure this party.

Things had cooled between Paloma and me and I was a little bit interested in a mate's sister, Rosie, who was sixteen and very pretty.

Paloma came to the party. I remember what she was wearing – a pair of white bell bottoms and a short blue and white sailor top. She'd put on weight, the bell bottoms were very tight around her hips, and her tummy bulged over the waist. Not a good look. I think her parents were having problems, though she hadn't confided in me. Her dad wasn't home much. Her mother never liked me; she'd never trusted me.

That night we hid bottles of beer and spirits in the choko vine. It was dark on the side of the yard shaded by the pigeon loft and the bottles were well hidden from my mother's watchful gaze, as she stood on the back steps that led down from the laundry. In the laundry we had bottles of Coke and Fanta in the tub with ice. Dad offered me a cigarette from his pack as he turned over the sausages and I had to pretend I'd never smoked one before. Mum handed out paper plates and serviettes and guided everyone to the table to pick up a slice of bread, a spoonful of potato salad, a squirt of tomato sauce and finally move on to the barbecue, where Dad put some meat on everyone's plates.

With Mum's back turned and Dad focused on his barbecue tongs, I saw Paloma tip a bottle of vodka into the punch and wink at me. She then tossed the empty bottle over the fence.

'Where did you get that from?' I asked.

'Dad's cocktail cabinet.' She grinned.

'But won't he notice?'

'He's not around much and, anyway, I don't think he ever drinks the stuff. It's mainly for visitors. I can fill it up again with water. Looks the same.'

She joined the food line and I stubbed out my cigarette and followed her.

'Where's your dad?'

'Dunno. Don't care.' She shrugged.

I was surprised, because she'd adored her father when we were younger. He used to be her hero.

My parents retreated inside after the food, birthday cake and unwrapping of presents, and we turned the music up as loud as my little record player would go, and we danced. I was starting to enjoy myself.

Paloma didn't dance, though. She was by the punchbowl, watching me and Rosie and drinking cup after cup of punch, and when the level in the bowl got low, someone else topped it up with brandy.

Then we all started swinging on the arms of the rotary clothes line. My parents wouldn't be pleased as they bent with our weight, but after a few beers, I didn't really care. Us guys lifted the girls up onto the arms and spun the clothes line faster and faster.

'I can fly,' Paloma squealed. Then she peed her pants.

I felt embarrassed for her and helped her down. Everyone was laughing at her. I thought she might go home, but she staggered towards the punchbowl and dipped the ladle in for another cup. She was very drunk.

A little while later, she was throwing up in the choko vine and everyone avoided her. I don't think she had any friends, apart from me, and I was having too much fun with Rosie to be bothered with her.

The party ended at midnight and some of the parents came to pick up their sons and daughters. Rosie's parents didn't come because she only lived a couple of blocks away and her big brother was supposed to take her home. He got the message, though, and went on ahead. I'd forgotten about Paloma and just assumed she'd gone home after being sick. Well, it was her fault, I thought. She should have known better.

I had my arm around Rosie's shoulders and we fell into step as we walked down the side of our house. I was thinking how marvellous it was that our bodies fitted together so neatly. I was tall, she was tiny, and I'd had to bend down to kiss her, but as we walked side by side her head was just under my armpit, her arm around my back, with her thumb hooked into the belt of my jeans.

Then I tripped on something and fell, dragging Rosie down with me. It was Paloma's leg. She was lying face down spreadeagled, half on the lawn and half in the azaleas.

'Fuck. What are you doing here?' I asked her.

'Flying,' she said. 'But it's no good. Everything's spinning. I want it to stop.' She got up on all fours and vomited on the grass.

'Leave her alone,' said Rosie, who had got to her feet and was tugging at me to stand up. 'She's disgusting.'

And that's what I did. I left Paloma alone and strode out on the street with little Rosie snuggling into my chest.

Next morning, the pigeons were released and I figured Paloma must have opened their loft. I staggered out of bed with my first hangover and nearly threw up when Mum gave me bacon and eggs for breakfast.

The doorbell rang and it was Paloma's mother, wanting to know if her daughter was still here.

'No,' I said. 'I thought she'd gone home. She was...she wasn't feeling well.'

'Well, she's not in her room. Is she in yours?' her mother asked.

My mother gasped.

My father stepped forward. 'I would never allow my son to have a girl in his room,' he said.

'It's all right, Dad.' I didn't want a row. 'No, she's not in my room. You can come and check if you don't believe me.'

Her mother blushed. 'It's all right. I'll take your word for it.'

'Maybe she's gone for a walk,' my mother suggested. 'I'm sure she'll be all right.'

'Paloma never walks unless she has to,' her mother said. 'Did you notice if she was with anyone at the party? A boy perhaps? She didn't go off with some strange boy, did she?'

'I don't think so,' I said.

My father was shaking his head. 'We got most of the parents to pick up their children, apart from you and Rosie's parents, because you're so close. I didn't think there would be a problem.'

'And we kept a good eye on the children. There was no hanky-panky, if that's what you're implying,' said my mother.

'No, no, of course I'm not. I'm sorry. It's just that, because of her leg and her other problems, you know…' Her mother looked close to tears.

'I'm sure she'll be home soon,' I said, thinking I'd have a look for her myself in the garden. Maybe she was still in the azaleas and no one had noticed. I was starting to feel a bit guilty about last night.

I checked the azaleas and choko vine and behind the loo, where the garden was a bit of a tangle. And while her mother was down the street talking to Rosie's parents, I went into her garden and checked the fig tree, because it occurred to me that Paloma was good at climbing, very strong in her arms for a girl, and we used to play in the tree when we were younger. It had grown since those days, and I thought it unlikely, but I still checked.

That afternoon, the police came to talk to me. Paloma was still missing and her mother feared she'd been abducted. Mum made the officers a cup of tea and we all sat in the living room on the good chairs.

'When was the last time you saw this crippled girl from next door?' I was asked.

'She's not exactly crippled,' I answered. 'She gets around quite well really. It's just one leg. She had polio.'

'She was at the party last night?'

'Yes.'

'And you told her mother that she wasn't feeling well.'

'Yep. And I just thought she'd gone home.'

'Why wasn't she feeling well?'

I shrugged.

'There was nothing wrong with the sausages,' my mother volunteered. 'No one else was sick.'

'There was no alcohol?'

'No. No. Definitely not.' My father said.

I noticed they wouldn't even admit to the Porphyry Pearl in the punch.

'Are you sure?' the officer asked. 'Because we found an empty bottle of vodka next door near the fence.'

'And we'd like to check your garden too, if you don't mind,' said the other officer.

I took them outside while Mum and Dad took the tea tray to the kitchen. I didn't want my parents to witness what would happen next.

I stood under the clothes line while the officers went straight to the choko vine. Glass clattered as they dug beer bottles and one brandy bottle out from under the vine, holding each up for me to see before depositing it in a box.

'They're not from last night,' I said. 'They've been there for ages.'

But my parents were standing next to me by now, also watching, and the officers clearly didn't believe me.

'How much did Paloma drink?'

I shrugged.

My mother looked horrified, and my father angry. I thought I'd rather go to jail than face my parents.

With the evidence on the front porch, the officers then wanted to search the house. I showed them my room. They turned on the lights, checked inside the wardrobe and under the bed. I was asked again if I had any idea where Paloma might be, and then they left, forgetting to take the empties with them.

My father brought the box inside. 'Where did these bottles come from?' he demanded.

'I don't know. I guess some of the guys brought them.'

'And you're going to try and tell me you didn't know anything about it.'

'Well, I am eighteen. I haven't broken any law.'

'Serving alcohol to minors is against the law.'

'And who put the plonk in the punch?' I asked, looking at my mother. My head was throbbing.

'You're grounded, son.'

'Grounded? I'm not a kid.'

'While you live in this house, you'll live by our rules. Now go to your room.' He stood blocking the front door.

'Get out of my way.'

He wouldn't move. I raised my fist and punched him on the face. I didn't know I was going to hit my father until I'd done it. It was that fast. I was shaking with the shock of it.

He wasn't. He grabbed my hands. My mother was tugging my shirt.

He pushed me away. 'Go to your room,' he said, 'and don't come out until you can behave like an adult.'

I stumbled into my room and slammed the door. The mirror that was hanging behind it fell off and shattered. I flung myself onto my bed, angry and confused, and regretting hitting my father. He was a big man, and I was sure he'd win a fight if he had a mind to. But I couldn't imagine it. He'd never even smacked me as a child, though I often deserved it. He'd threaten but never did, and I learned to take no notice of his threats. I'd received some gentle smacks from Mum occasionally, which hurt my self-esteem more than my backside.

If I really wanted to get out of the house, I didn't need to use the front door. I just had to step outside my window. I pulled up the blind and stared out at Paloma's backyard, and there she was on the roof of the pigeon loft, straddling the ridge as if she were riding a horse. She saw me and waved furiously. A branch from the fig tree overhung the loft and I realised she must have crawled along it and lowered herself down onto the roof.

Now she was stuck, since the branch, without her weight on it, had sprung up out of her reach. The roof was corrugated iron, and it was a hot day. The first thing she asked for when I rescued her with my father's ladder was a glass of water.

3

We sold our old house and rented a unit in the same block as Paloma for six months while the new house was being built. I began to sleep better, but it was strange to think that Paloma was just two floors below us.

We saw her quite often. Paloma was using a walking frame now, and seemed to be suffering much more pain. Barbara told me Paloma had confided to her that she had post-polio syndrome, which was a new one on me. It was impossible for her to walk the dog, and Barbara offered to do it. Sometimes I went too, but the little beast didn't seem to like me – only women and children, apparently. We often took Toby with us when we visited the site and he made friends with the neighbour's little boy. Since I'd finished the fence, they could both run around our neighbour's backyard in safety.

One day we returned Toby to Paloma and found her on the floor, unable to get back on her feet. She didn't seem to be injured, and she told us it had happened only a few minutes before we arrived, though I'm not sure I believed her. Barbara and I managed to get her up again, and onto a lounge chair. Toby jumped up onto her lap and licked away her tears.

Barbara pushed the walker in front of her chair, and found some tissues for her.

'It was my silly fault,' Paloma said, blowing her nose. 'I forgot to put the brake on this contraption, and when I tried to stand up it zipped away from under me. Never mind, lesson learned.'

'Maybe we should take you to the doctor,' I suggested, 'just to check you're okay.'

'No, no, no. I'm fine.' She shook her head and waved her hand. 'What's he going to do anyway? Put me in a home?' She laughed and put Toby back on the floor. 'I need to go to the bathroom,' she said, pulling herself up from her chair and grabbing the handles of the walker.

Barbara and I both moved to steady her, but she was on her way, pushing the walker in front of her, with her jaw clenched tight and that look of determination I remembered from her childhood. There was no arguing with her when she had that look.

She opened the bathroom door wide. 'See! Safety rails everywhere. I'll be okay. You don't have to worry about me.' Then she turned towards me, one hand leaning on the door frame, and flung the other arm around my neck. She kissed me on the cheek. 'Thank you.'

We left her in the bathroom, calling through the door for her to ring us if she needed anything, and closed the front door behind us so Toby wouldn't escape. Paloma never locked her front door, claiming she'd forgotten where she'd put the key; and anyway, she'd added, Toby always barked when there were strangers around. He hardly ever barked these days.

We lived in that top-floor unit for almost six months. In that time, Barbara and I shopped for carpets and appliances together and chose paint colours for the walls. I was less worried about our finances. Barbara told me she was relieved that we were doing things together again, and I realised that I must have been a bit difficult to live with before we'd sold the house.

We both worried about Paloma. Barbara would often stay for a cup of tea after her walks with Toby, and she was distressed to learn that Paloma was completely alone: no cousins, uncles, aunts or any other relatives. Paloma worried about Toby if anything were to happen to her, and was frightened to go to the doctor in case he gave her bad news or wanted to put her into a nursing home.

That childish peck on the cheek, the way she flung her arm around me as we followed her to the bathroom on the day of her fall disturbed me. It shouldn't have, I know. The innocence of it reminded me of Paloma as a young girl with that crooked grin.

Moving day came, and Paloma watched from her doorway as the removalists took our furniture from the unit. Most of our heavier furniture had been kept in a storage unit while we waited for the house to be finished, so it didn't take the removalists long. Who would take Toby for his walks now? I hoped someone nice would move into the unit we had just vacated, someone who liked little dogs. I tried to convince myself, and Barbara, that it wasn't our problem. Barbara promised she'd call in for a chat whenever she went shopping.

A few days later, when we'd finally unpacked all the boxes and filled the cupboards and wardrobes with all our stuff, Barbara decided she was missing our grandchildren, who were living interstate. Usually we visited them, but with the construction work we hadn't actually seen them for over a year – apart from on Skype.

'Wouldn't it be nice to have them all here?' she suggested.

'All at once?' I loved our grandchildren, but preferred them in small doses. 'There's only two spare rooms, and one of them is my study.'

'We'll manage. We've still got that old tent, you know. We could put it up in the backyard. They'd love it.'

'Surely it's full of holes,' I argued.

'Well, let's see.'

And so we dragged the tent out of the cupboard in the garage. It was a large tent, and we'd had some great camping trips with our boys when they were young, but it had to be at least twenty years old now.

We erected it in our backyard, and our neighbours watched the performance over the new paling fence, offering advice here and there. Having an audience turned it into a bit of a game.

'What's the matter with your bedroom?' my neighbour joked.

'We're thinking of having our grandkids here,' Barbara explained.

Instead of arguing, we burst out laughing when it fell down. Two poles were missing and we took turns holding parts up while the other inspected the canvas. There were a few holes, but it was in better condition than I had expected.

'They don't make them like this nowadays,' I said.

'It'll be okay if we put a large tarpaulin over it,' said Barbara, 'or pray it doesn't rain.'

'And I'm sure we can buy a few more poles,' I said, finding myself enthusiastic for the project.

'Okay,' said Barbara, dropping her end of the tent. 'Let's go Skype the kids.'

They all came for Christmas and the noise was incredible. We had four small folk and four extra adults in our open-plan house, and the sound seemed to reverberate off the walls. Mostly happy sounds. Thank goodness for the tent, where our grandchildren seemed to want to play most of the time.

We had a family Christmas, with lots of toys for the children, and everyone pitched in with the food preparation. It was a great day.

On Boxing Day, we asked Paloma and Toby, and some of our neighbours, over for lunch, which was to be mostly leftovers and sausages on the barbecue for children. Our youngest grandson and the little chap from next door were both three and they spent a lot of time together at our place. His mother was very pregnant and glad to have him off her hands for a while. Barbara and I watched from the front yard as the children and quite a few parents played a game of cricket on the road. It was a quiet street, hardly any cars, especially on a holiday. Someone put some traffic cones down to warn any motorists who might drive by.

Paloma was in a wheelchair now, and Barbara had driven over to her place to pick her up. Toby loved the children but had given up chasing the ball after a short while and gone next door.

I was feeling nostalgic, enjoying the day: the beer, the sunshine, the cricket.

Then Barbara was beside me saying something about water being broken. I thought there was something wrong with the plumbing and it took a while to understand what she was talking about.

'He's taking her to hospital,' she said. 'She's having the baby. And can we watch their boy.'

'One more won't make any difference,' I said, realising she was talking about our neighbours.

I heard the car start up next door, the whine of it reversing down the driveway, then a scream.

'Toby!' It was Paloma. She flung herself out of her wheelchair and fell onto the ground. Everyone gathered around her. The car was hidden by the paling fence.

I thought it might be one of the children at first, under the car. But it was Toby.

Our neighbours had a little girl, born a few hours later. Their joy however was tainted by guilt, and they offered to bury Toby in their backyard, which, after all, had been his puppyhood home.

Toby was kept cool in an esky while our children and grandchildren, who were still staying with us, decorated a cardboard box with pictures – some drawn, some cut from magazines – and we used it for his coffin. Paloma lined it with Toby's favourite blanket. As my son-in-law said, it was a good opportunity for the children to learn about death and celebrate a life.

We held a proper funeral service, which was surprisingly well-attended by local families, burying Toby near the fence I'd built. The children who had played with Toby took turns to say something about the games they played, some needing prompting from their parents. Paloma had a small brass plaque engraved which was nailed to the fence. Barbara made cakes and biscuits and there were jugs of fruit juice for the children. I couldn't help but be moved by the service, and felt foolish wiping tears from my eyes as we lowered Toby's coffin into the ground. After the children had finished with the cake and biscuits, we wheeled Paloma into our house for something stronger. I thought she was coping well, considering, but she was always much stronger than you'd expect.

*

We hadn't heard from Paloma for a number of days after Toby's funeral. Barbara had phoned twice before going shopping early in the New Year, planning to drop in on her, but there'd been no answer.

'Where could she be?' Barbara asked after phoning again that evening.

'Perhaps she's gone away somewhere,' I suggested.

'Where would she go? In a wheelchair!'

'Just because she's in a wheelchair, doesn't mean she…'

'Don't be silly.'

'Maybe she's just not answering the phone. Maybe she just doesn't feel like talking to people.'

Barbara picked up the car keys. 'We're going over there. Come on.'

We found a parking spot outside her block of units, and I followed Barbara into the foyer. The door to her unit was closed, but not locked. We turned on the lights as we entered. Called her name.

'I heard something, didn't you?' Barbara said, as we walked across the dining room.

I noticed the hallstand and the big table had gone, probably because she needed more space for her wheelchair. 'Paloma? Are you there?'

'Here. In the bedroom. Oh, help me.'

We turned on the bedroom light and there she was, on the floor.

It looked as if she'd fallen out of bed, as the bedclothes had been dragged with her, and she was tangled in them. There was blood on her forehead. I bent down to examine the wound.

'I'll call an ambulance,' said Barbara, pulling out her phone. 'Don't move her.'

'Oh, John, I'm sorry.' Her voice was soft, I had to lean close to hear. She grabbed my arm.

'How long have you been like this?' I asked, as Barbara gave the address to the operator.

'Don't know. Got a terrible headache.' She closed her eyes, released her grip on my arm.

It only took five minutes for the ambulance to arrive – I know because I checked my watch every few seconds as I paced the footpath outside the units. Barbara stayed with Paloma.

When they pulled up, parked behind our car, I told them they'd need a stretcher, and held doors open as they entered the unit. Then Barbara and I waited outside the bedroom while they checked her and lifted her onto the trolley. We followed the trolley out to the ambulance and learned where they would be taking her.

Barbara, bless her, is so efficient in an emergency. She gathered together some of Paloma's personal belongings – clean underwear, her hairbrush, toothbrush and toothpaste – before getting into our car and driving to the hospital. I pulled the door to her unit closed. It was a good thing she never locked her front door.

Questions, questions, questions.

'Next of kin?'

'None.'

'Family doctor?'

Barbara thought he was the same doctor we saw, but wasn't sure.

'Previous illnesses?'

'Polio.'

'Previous surgery?'

'The lip,' I said, 'and some operations on her legs after polio, when she was a child.'

'Allergies?'

'No idea.'

'So, you are…?'

'John and Barbara Higgins. Close friends, I guess. Neighbours.'

'Ah, she mentioned you, I think. She's having some scans at the moment but you can see her when they've finished.'

'Is she going to be okay?' I asked.

'You'll have to speak to her doctor.'

We waited by her bed for the doctor. Paloma seemed to be comfortable but was drifting in and out of consciousness, mumbling to herself occasionally, not making any sense. They'd put a drip into her arm to rehydrate her, so I guess she'd been on the bedroom floor for some time.

A bleed on the brain, the doctor told us when he finally came in. He asked again if we were sure she had no next of kin.

'Positive,' I said. 'She had a dog, Toby, who she absolutely adored, treated like a child.'

The doctor smiled. He was a young chap, who probably wouldn't understand.

'He died just about a week ago, so if she's talking about someone called Toby…'

'No, it's not that. It's just that she has a scar on her abdomen, which looks like a scar from a caesarean. But perhaps it's something else. Or perhaps the child didn't survive.'

Barbara and I looked at each other. I shook my head.

Barbara said, 'I actually asked her once and she definitely said she had no family. Because we were worried about her living on own, especially as she got less able to move around.'

'She told us she had post-polio syndrome.' I added.

Barbara washed the sheets and made the bed while I went around the unit with carpet cleaner and a vacuum to try to get rid of the smell of stale urine. There was no one else to do it and we weren't aware of any official documents she might have put in place in case something like this happened.

Barbara contacted our doctor's surgery and asked if Paloma was a patient there, but they wouldn't tell us because we weren't next of kin. So she told them anyway that Paloma had been taken to hospital in an ambulance last night. Later we received a phone call from our doctor who assured us that he had been contacted by the hospital and that he had given them details of her various health issues.

'All this red tape and concern about privacy, when all we're trying to do is help,' said Barbara. 'Heaven help us if we have to contact her lawyer.'

'If she has one.'

'Who would know?'

The next day while we were searching her unit again for any paperwork that would give us these answers, they performed surgery on Paloma to relieve the pressure on her brain. No one told us it was about to happen, and so we were surprised when we drove out to the hospital to see her, and found her bed empty. No one knew where she was. Someone thought she was still in surgery, someone else thought they'd moved her to another ward. But because we weren't next of kin…they weren't really allowed to…

Barbara exploded! I felt sorry for the poor nurse who had delivered this last piece of non-information.

'Don't you understand! Don't you care!' she yelled. 'She has no family. We're all she's got. Is this what happens to people if they have no one to speak up for them?'

I put my arm around Barbara and tried to drag her away.

'I think someone came from the Salvation Army last night,' said the nurse.

'It doesn't matter.' She pulled away from me and strode down the corridor wiping tears from her eyes.

I had to run to catch up with her.

In the car, I suggested we go and see our doctor. Surely he'd know what's going on. We didn't make an appointment. We went straight there, asked to see him, urgently, and took a seat in the waiting room. Barbara wasn't moving until she had some answers.

He told us that they had performed surgery on Paloma to relieve the pressure on her brain, and she had died on the operating table.

*

I spoke to someone from the body corporate at Paloma's block of units and told him the news. He would put a note in everyone's letter box, because they all knew Paloma. Then he asked me about her funeral, and what would happen about the unit.

'Goodness knows. She doesn't have any family, so I'm not sure what happens. I don't know if she made a will, if she's got a lawyer or anything!' Barbara and I had been discussing it.

'There's a chap who used to live here who's a retired lawyer. In a nursing home now. I'll ask him. I think they were friends.'

*

Some questions were answered the following day when I received a phone call from George Faraday. I had to listen carefully as his voice was very soft. I pictured a frail elderly man.

'I've just heard that poor Paloma has died,' he said. 'I used to live in the units near her and I helped her draw up her will,' he explained.

'Well, thank you for getting in touch with us,' I said. 'We were wondering about that.'

'I've got a copy here, and you're mentioned in it. I really should talk to you face to face, but there are a couple of things you need to know. The first is, she'd already paid for her funeral. Have you got a pen and paper handy?'

I reached across the kitchen bench and grabbed the shopping list Barbara was compiling, and he dictated the details.

'The next thing is, who's looking after Toby?'

'Toby? Oh, he died, I'm afraid. Boxing Day. Under a car…'

'Oh, that's sad. She must have been heartbroken. She adored that dog.' His voice faded and he seemed to be talking to someone in the background. 'Sorry about that. One of the nurses wants me to take a pill. I'm in a nursing home now. Body's not too good, but I hope my brain's in better nick. Hang on a minute.'

I heard the phone being put down, and muffled conversation, and while I waited for him to come back to me, I told Barbara what the call was about.

'Are you still there?' he asked.

'Yes.'

'Paloma updated her will about a year ago,' he said. 'It was after she met you and your wife, Barbara. She told me you were old friends and was very excited to renew the friendship. I had drawn up the original will, while I was still practising as a lawyer, and in the original will she wanted to leave everything to charities.'

'That doesn't surprise me.'

'But she was always worried about what would happen to Toby if she died before him, and she knew she wasn't well. So, when she updated her will, she requested that you and your wife, Barbara, be responsible for Toby's care, and she'd specified a very generous amount of money for that purpose. Did she discuss it with you? She promised she would.'

'Not really, although I knew she worried about Toby.'

'I suppose it's not relevant now.'

'No.'

'You'll need to get in touch with a lawyer. I mean, someone who isn't on death's doorstep like me. Do you have a family solicitor?'

I gave him our solicitor's details, and he said he'd contact him and send a copy of the will. Meanwhile, I would contact the funeral home and organise the funeral. He gave me his details, and I promised I'd keep him updated on the arrangements.

We hadn't expected a crowd, but I was distressed to see only seven people turn up for Paloma's funeral. Three were women, sitting on the opposite side of the chapel, two in the second row and one behind them. I thought I recognised them from Toby's burial. An elderly gentleman was wheeled in by a younger woman and he parked himself near us, then introduced himself – George Faraday – to Barbara and me. His attendant was his daughter, and she slid into the pew next to us.

A couple of weeks ago, we'd buried Toby in our neighbour's backyard with about twenty people participating. Most, I suppose, were children, and it was turned into a bit of a game for them. A grown-up's funeral was different. It was still school summer holidays and no doubt parents who might have wanted to come had to organise child-minding and so on. Our neighbours had apologised for not coming today because he was back at work and she was struggling to cope with a newborn and a toddler.

Paloma had wanted a non-religious service, so it was led by a celebrant in a chapel at the crematorium. She'd specified 'Wind Beneath My Wings' by Bette Midler for music and something more upbeat for the end of the service, so I chose Dean Martin singing 'La Paloma'. She was brought into the chapel in the *cheapest coffin possible,* as per her wishes. It was white and lacking decoration apart from a bunch of Australian native flowers on top. She had actually specified cardboard in her instructions but that wasn't acceptable to the funeral directors. She had also left instructions for her ashes to be spread *somewhere high, where she could take off and fly.*

At our meeting with the celebrant, Barbara and I had volunteered to say a few words. When it came to actually writing those few words, I wanted to back down. How was I going to do this? I felt racked by guilt. Would I tell the truth? That Paloma was my first love? I kissed her when I was fifteen. And later I abandoned her. Worse, I flaunted my freedom in front of her – a freedom she would never have. I remembered my eighteenth birthday party, when I left her vomiting in the bushes while I trotted off with Rosie. Paloma's mother was right for not trusting me, though we never did anything more than heavy petting.

I remembered a night after I'd moved out of home and was flatting with some other students while I was at uni. I came home once a fortnight or so for dinner with my folks and I usually had a load of washing to do. I'd stay the night, take my washing home in the morning, usually only half-dry and heavy as I lugged it to the station for the train ride back to the flat.

One night she'd come over the fence, appearing suddenly beside me in the laundry. She'd seen me from her place. It was quite late for a casual visit. She was trembling. It was cold and she was only wearing a nightie. Bare feet. My parents had gone to bed, and I was conscious of not waking them.

'What's the matter?' I'd asked.

'Nothing.'

'Well, what do you want?'

'Just wanted to say hi. Just wanted to know how you are.'

'Yep. I'm good. Uni's good. Getting good marks.'

I should have asked her about herself, but the washing machine had finished and I busied myself with pulling clothes out of it. Mum had set up a drying rack in the laundry, because of the pigeons, and I draped my clothes over it. The two of us in the room made it difficult because there wasn't much space. She was in my way.

'Sorry,' she'd said. 'I can see you're busy. I shouldn't have come.'

She waited a few minutes, obviously hoping I'd say something nice to her – but I didn't. I didn't even look at her. She was sniffling, probably crying. I just didn't want to get involved, and if I put my arms around her, said anything comforting, I knew I would be. She shrugged and turned round and limped down the steps.

Sitting in the chapel, while the celebrant told the small group about Paloma's courage and love for animals and children, I was struggling.

What would people think of me if I told the truth? I couldn't. And, when I looked at the small congregation, I wondered if there was any point in saying anything.

By the time Bette Midler sang '*Did you know that you're my hero*', I was weeping. Barbara handed me a bunch of tissues, and I focused on getting myself under control, so I could read what I'd prepared. It was just a brief outline of her childhood and teenage years, and Barbara was to cover her more recent past.

Standing in front of the group, I kept my eyes on my page of handwritten notes. I told the gathering that I'd first met Paloma when we were both about five, that she was the girl next door, that we were both only children and playmates.

'We grew up together,' I said. 'She was unlucky in health, and often in hospital. But she was the bravest kid I'd ever met. She never complained, never let it get her down.'

I looked up, focused my eyes briefly on Barbara, because I had a weird sensation that Paloma was there – in front of me, listening to what I was saying about her. If I'd been standing in front of a crowd, I could have avoided looking directly at anyone, but with only six people I didn't want to meet anyone else's eyes, so I blinked away the threatening tears and looked down again at the words on the page.

'She always wanted to fly,' I read, 'and she was called Paloma because her father thought she was like a little dove. I wanted to…' I cleared my throat, which was suddenly husky. 'I wanted to teach her to fly, and for much of our time together as children it was our favourite game. We'd pretend we could fly. We'd practise – climbing trees, jumping off, trying to catch each other as we'd fall, usually crashing to the ground and collecting bruises and scratches. We collected *Superman* comics, and sometimes she'd be Lois Lane and I'd be Clark Kent.'

I looked towards Barbara again and saw she was smiling. Encouraged, I continued. 'Eventually, we grew up and stopped playing these games. I was like a big brother to Paloma, I guess, but we lost contact when I went on to university. I moved away from home, finished my degree and met Barbara and only saw Paloma occasionally when I went home to my parents' place. She went to business college, learned shorthand and typing and was working as a secretary when my parents sold their home and moved away. And I'm afraid I don't know much about her life between her late teens and when we met again about a year ago. So here I'm going to hand over to Barbara, who spent some time with Paloma recently.'

I turned and faced the coffin. I'd planned to say something like 'We'll miss you, Paloma', but the words caught in my throat and wouldn't come out.

Then Barbara was beside me, with her page of neatly typed notes. She gave me a hug and I went back to my seat, feeling relieved that that was over.

Barbara read, 'I got to know Paloma quite well in the brief time I knew her. She became increasingly disabled in her last year and couldn't take Toby for walks, so I helped out with that and a bit of shopping, and we'd have a cuppa and a chat. I was curious to know about her life, and she was curious to know about mine, especially the romantic parts – how I met John, all about our wedding, our children and so on, and over the last few months she became like one of the family. She did tell me that John was the first boy she ever kissed, and that there hadn't been many others. We worried about her, but she seemed happy.'

Barbara talked about Toby, and filled in some gaps she'd learned about Paloma's career, her various jobs, as a secretary and a bookkeeper. Unlike me, Barbara seemed to be in good control of her emotions.

The celebrant took over again, and read a poem by Mary Frye, chosen by Paloma: 'Do not stand at my grave and weep, I am not there…'

As her coffin slid behind the curtains, where it would wait in a queue before being taken to the furnace, we all stood. I still had the feeling Paloma was there, though, watching me, and as I walked down the aisle, I glanced at the three women who had also attended the service. One of them was Paloma. A much younger Paloma, about fifty, without a limp or a harelip. There was no doubt in my mind.

This Paloma began speaking to me. She said. 'Hi, John, I've been looking for you for a long time. I believe you're my father.'

I slumped against a pillar. Barbara gasped. I felt everyone looking at me. The sun was too hot. For a minute, I thought I was about to have a heart attack, and someone found me a chair.

4

We hadn't planned on having a wake but the small group gathered at our place after the service. Barbara had driven me home, as I was in a bit of a state. I kept telling her it was impossible because I'd never had sex with Paloma, unless it was some sort of immaculate conception! I was sure the woman – Jenny was her name – was some sort of nutcase or had a hidden agenda.

I poured drinks for everyone: Jenny, my alleged daughter; George Faraday and his daughter; Barbara and myself. We clinked glasses and drank a toast to Paloma. Then I sank into the lounge, exhausted. I felt awful, and put my glass down after a token sip.

Barbara had managed to find some cheese and crackers and olives, and she put them on the coffee table and told everyone to take a seat and help themselves. She sat next to me, put her reassuring hand on my knee. In the car she'd told me it was a bit of a shock, but wasn't worried about it because, after all, it was a long time ago and we'd both had relationships and slept with other people before we met each other. Clearly, she didn't believe my denials.

Jenny was slightly built with fair hair like Paloma's, and full lips, and could have been attractive twenty years ago. I noticed her hands. She was a nail-biter, and there was a small tattoo on the inside of her wrist. I don't know why I thought of it, but I remembered reading something about people getting tattoos to hide scars. Something about her made me feel uneasy. I wanted to ask her how she managed to find Paloma, but didn't want to be the first person to say anything.

George eventually broke the silence, addressing Jenny. 'You look very like your mother when she was younger. Do you know for sure that you are her daughter?'

'I have my birth certificate.' She put her wine down and rummaged in her purse, blushing slightly as she did, which also reminded me of Paloma. Eventually she produced a plastic sleeve and passed it to me.

'Jenny Grey, date of birth July 1968' – the year I turned eighteen, the year I started uni and the year I moved into a flat. 'Mother's name Paloma Grey. Father's name John Higgins, student.' It was there in black and white. I passed the document to Barbara.

'How did you find Paloma?' I asked.

'Well, I always knew I was adopted. My mum and dad never tried to keep that from me, and besides, it was obvious – I don't look anything like them. They've both got brown eyes.' She studied my face. 'You've got brown eyes too, not green.'

'Paloma had green eyes,' said Barbara.

'It's not impossible for two brown-eyed parents to have a child with green eyes,' said George. 'But it is very rare.'

'I wish I could have seen her,' said Jenny. 'She sounds like a really nice person. Even if I only saw her from a distance. When I was a kid, I wanted to know what my birth mother was like. It's not to say I didn't love my mum and dad. I just felt so different. I pestered and pestered them. Then, it was just before I was about to get married, I asked my mum again and this time she told me...' She wiped her eyes and continued. 'This is going to sound awful, I know, and I don't necessarily believe it, but what my mum told me was that my birth mother was very young when she had me and that she was a cripple, and...'

'Not exactly a cripple,' I said, 'but she'd had polio as a baby and a bad leg.'

'Oh. I thought it might be something like that from what you said at the service. Did she have cancer?'

'No,' George answered. 'She died following a fall and had a cerebral haemorrhage – a bleed on the brain.'

'Oh, okay. I thought it might be cancer because I've had breast cancer and sometimes that runs in families. I'm okay now. So was it sudden?'

'Fairly sudden,' Barbara answered. 'I don't think she was in any pain at the end.'

'You were telling us how you found out who your mother was,' I reminded her.

'Yes, sorry. Well, that wasn't all Mum said about Paloma. Mum told me that the pregnancy was the consequence of a rape.'

I heard Barbara gasp beside me. 'John would never…'

'I don't necessarily believe everything Mum told me. It's just what she said, and for some reason or another she really didn't want me to find my birth mother. It might have been because she thought I might stop loving her or something, I don't know. Anyway, I sort of accepted that when I was younger and besides I was busy with my work and with a marriage that just wasn't what I expected, which ended up in divorce.'

'Do you have children?' asked Barbara. She looked hopeful.

'No. I couldn't have children. It's probably for the best, but I would have liked to have some.' She picked up her wine glass, looked at it, then put it back on the coffee table and wound a scrunched-up tissue around her fingers. 'Anyway, my parents have both died now. Dad died before Mum, and she passed away about two years ago. I'd already searched a lot of Mum's things – marriage certificate, her birth certificate, the title deeds to the house – and I didn't find anything, except some adoption papers, which had no mention of my birth parents' names. It was different in those days. Then one day I had this flash. There was a photo of me as a baby on the piano. It was framed. I was very young, about three months old, I think. Maybe it was my christening. I took it out of its frame and there it was – that birth certificate. It was the sort of thing Mum did – putting sentimental things in the picture frames.' She took a fresh tissue from the box and blew her nose. 'I wonder, do you have any photos of Paloma?'

'Yes, of course.' Barbara was on her feet. On the sideboard was a recent photo we'd taken of the whole family on Boxing Day before the accident, adults in the back row, children in the front row with Paloma in her wheelchair in the centre, and Toby on her lap. 'Sorry, it's not very good, but I'm sure there'll be others.'

Jenny put on her glasses and smiled at it.

'So, after you found your birth certificate, what did you do then?' I asked.

'Ah, this is the difficult part. At first I was really excited, especially when I saw her name, Paloma. Such an unusual name. I thought it'd be easy. But I didn't know if she'd married, and if she had, what her surname was. I thought she might have married you, so I searched for Paloma Higgins and Paloma Grey. And she could have changed her first name too, I thought. She might have hated being called Paloma. And then, on top of that, I had this feeling of dread, actually, because she probably didn't want me to find her. If she had been raped – sorry John, this is what I was thinking, because I didn't know – I thought she might be really upset about it, not want to be reminded of it, you know. And I could understand that. Did she ever say anything about having a child?'

'No, and we were keen to find out if she had any family. But,' Barbara looked at me, 'remember, there was a doctor who said she had a scar like a caesarean...'

I nodded.

'So I might have been a caesarean birth? That's interesting. And in those days they usually just took the baby away from unwed mothers, didn't they? She might not have even known if she had a boy or a girl. She would have been unconscious from the anaesthetic.'

'Very likely,' said Barbara.

'Fancy keeping something like that a secret for all those years,' said Jenny. 'How awful. Well, I got nowhere at Birth Deaths and Marriages. I paid for searches and there was no record of either Paloma Grey or Paloma Higgins having died, so I thought the chances were that she was still alive. Or that she wasn't a Grey or a Higgins. I just about wore out Google and Linked In and all those other search engines. And Facebook! Do you have any idea how many Greys and Higginses there are in New South Wales? I signed up to an ancestry website. I searched newspapers, made a habit of looking at the death notices. And then I saw the notice you must have put in the paper last weekend. And I thought, Wow! Of course I had to come to the funeral but I didn't know what I was going to do. And I'm sorry for the way I told you. It must have given you a shock.'

'That's a lot of work.' I was feeling a bit better. She was like the young Paloma in many ways – there was a restlessness, nervous energy perhaps, and the way she flicked the hair out of eyes. Her voice also, with a slight inflection at the end of every sentence, though she didn't have Paloma's harelip and her enunciation was clearer.

'You could say I was obsessed. But not knowing drove me crazy.'

'And it's so sad that you never met her,' said Barbara.

'What do you think she would have done if she'd known?'

George, who had been listening quietly to this story answered. 'I think it's right that you didn't get to meet her. Although I know that sounds a bit cruel.'

'Do you know something? Did she tell you anything?'

'Sorry, dear. No. And she did confide in me quite a lot,' he said. 'So, I can only think it was something that she was very ashamed of.'

'But she knew about me, didn't she, because she must have filled out some forms after she gave birth. What about her will?' Jenny asked. 'Did she leave a will? Maybe she's mentioned me.'

George shook his head. 'I think we'd better leave that to the proper authorities, I'm afraid. You'll need to see a solicitor.'

'Oh no, you've got it all wrong. I'm not after any sort of inheritance. I just want to know about my birth mother and why she didn't want to know about me. I hope you don't think...'

I interrupted. 'And why she put my name down as the father on that birth certificate. Because I'm not. I'm sorry, but I'm not your father.

I never slept with Paloma. I know you don't believe me.' I looked at Barbara and Jenny and sank back in the lounge.

George cleared his throat. 'For your name to be on a birth certificate as the father, you must have signed the form. Paloma would have been given a form to fill out in hospital to register the birth. Has to be done within a certain period of time, I can't remember how long. Or, perhaps Paloma signed a stat dec, explaining why you weren't around to sign the form.'

'Well, you won't find my signature on any forms relating to Jenny's birth. I know that. I'll make enquiries. I'll prove it! Damn it, I'll get my DNA tested. Would you be willing to have your DNA tested?' I asked Jenny.

'Sure! I'd be happy to do that.'

*

In order to prove my innocence, the next day I organised DNA testing for both myself and Jenny, at our expense. Barbara thought it was a waste of money, stressing again and again that it didn't matter. We both agreed there was no doubt Jenny was a close relation to Paloma – probably her daughter as she claimed she was. The kit would arrive in the mail and I'd let Jenny know when it arrived.

I also made an appointment to see our solicitor, Richard Law, and George was keen to accompany us, so the following day we picked him and his wheelchair up from the nursing home and drove into town, where we pushed him through the busy streets. We'd had some practice with Paloma, who was much heavier to push around than George. When we came to the seven steps in front of our solicitor's building, and no ramp, we discovered that George was capable of standing and pulling himself up them using a handrail and support from Barbara, while I bumped the wheelchair backwards up the steps.

I had hoped George would show us a copy of the will, but he wanted to leave it until we met with Richard.

Richard was the son of my father's solicitor, and his older brother was a good mate from my school days, who disappointed his father by becoming a musician. The Law Office, as it was known, was where it had been for almost a century, on the thirteenth floor, because the rent was cheapest there. I always dreaded going up in the lift, which smelled of damp wool, was slow and noisy and cramped with the three of us and the wheelchair.

Richard was a big man, a decade or so younger than us, and a heavy smoker, with a full ashtray always perched on the window ledge, and the window opened just a crack. His office always smelled of air freshener which didn't quite do its job.

Stacks of files littered the floor, and we had to move them into a corner before the three of us could arrange chairs around his desk, leaving the wheelchair folded in the corridor because it wouldn't fit. No doubt when George was practising law he'd have had the use of a conference room, with a polished table and plenty of chairs. I felt a bit embarrassed as I introduced George to Richard, because I imagined George would not be impressed, and we all shook Richard's pudgy, nicotine-stained hand.

As he rummaged amongst the paperwork on his desk, he asked us how we were enjoying the new house, the conveyancing being the last bit of business we'd done with him. Eventually he discovered the folder marked Paloma Grey, tucked his shirt back into his trousers and sat down.

'Well, this is a bit like winning the lottery, isn't it?' he said, pushing his glasses onto his nose. 'Now that the dog has died.'

'I don't know,' I said, shaking my head. 'We don't know what's in the will.'

'Oh, I see. I thought Paloma would have discussed things with you. She obviously thought a lot of you. And I gather that the will was changed recently.'

'That's right,' said George. 'I drew up the original will and made the changes last year.'

'In a nutshell, then,' Richard continued, 'you stand to inherit quite a bit. I'm not sure what the unit is worth – maybe a few hundred thousand?'

'About $400,000, I should think,' said George.

'Then she left about half a million to the dog, with you as trustees, and when the dog died, the amount remaining was to be used by you at your discretion.'

'Goodness, that's…' said Barbara.

'…and there's more. There's some shares – not sure of the value at this stage – but they'd give you a tidy dividend…'

'I had no idea…' I said, looking at Barbara. 'Did you?'

'No,' said Barbara, 'I thought she was living on a pension.'

'And there are other specified amounts to go to various charities.' He grinned, and sat back in his chair, which seemed to groan as it took his weight.

'Yes,' said George, 'but there might be a complication. I think there's a possibility the will could be challenged.'

'By Jenny?' I asked.

'Yes, by Jenny, who claims to be John's and Paloma's daughter. She turned up at the funeral and showed us her birth certificate, which seems genuine.'

'There's no mention of any next of kin,' said Richard, 'just the dog, Toby.'

'That's right, this is completely out of the blue,' said George.

'And that birth certificate has got to be a fake,' I butted in. 'I'm not Jenny's father, but how do I go about proving that it's a fake. There must be ways we can check. I knew nothing about Paloma having a baby – if she had one.' It suddenly seemed very hot in the crowded office, and I pulled a handkerchief from my pocket and wiped my forehead.

'There's DNA these days,' Richard suggested.

'I've already sent off for a kit.'

'And she's willing to do that?'

I nodded.

'Might not stand up in court,' he added.

'I know that. And I think that's okay at this stage. But what really intrigues me – actually, makes me very angry – is this wretched birth certificate naming me as the father.' I was sweating a lot and feeling a bit out of breath.

'Don't worry, we can find out. I can organise it if you like. A little bit of money involved doing those sorts of searches, but you can afford it.' He smiled. 'Generally you can find the original documents through Births Deaths and Marriages. Do you have a copy of the certificate?'

'Yes.' Barbara had taken a photo of it on her phone when we'd met Jenny and she had managed to get it printed on our home printer. She pulled the page from her purse and handed it to Richard.

He lifted some files from the lid of a photocopier under the window in his office, and placed the document on its glass plate, then pressed some buttons and another copy of the birth certificate slid out of it onto the floor. A copy of a copy, and it looked just as good as the original. It's so easy these days to fake things.

Then Barbara said, 'You know, if she is your daughter, then I think she deserves to have everything... I don't understand why you're so sure...'

'Because she's not! She's lying.' I found myself standing. I was shouting at Barbara. My shirt felt very tight.

'It's okay.' George signalled to me to sit down. 'We'll get this sorted.'

Barbara continued. 'Really, we didn't expect to inherit anything. It's more than we need. It just doesn't seem fair, that's all.' She looked at me. 'Are you all right?'

'A glass of water,' I said, sitting down. I wasn't feeling well, but didn't want to make a fuss. I'd had anxiety attacks before.

Richard left the room and returned with a glass of water.

*

The next few weeks were busy. We had Paloma's unit to sell, but first we had to empty it and make decisions on what was to be kept, what was to be thrown and what should be taken to Vinnies. Having moved house twice in the last two years, we were experts at it.

Barbara disappeared into Paloma's bedroom to empty wardrobes while I attended to books and music on the shelves in the living room. I wanted to throw out almost all of Paloma's books, which were mainly cheap paperback romances. Barbara, however, was of the opinion that Vinnies would love them – in fact, she thought Paloma had probably bought them from Vinnies.

There were some good books that I thought worth keeping, if only to hand them down to our grandchildren. I recognised some of them. There was a book I had given her – Captain W.E. Johns, *Wings of Romance*. I blushed when I saw what I had written inside – *One day, we'll fly away together*, and my very childish signature and a couple of kisses in the form of crosses. I must have been about twelve. There were other Biggles books that she'd kept all these years, many of them given to her by her parents. She was a big fan. I decided to keep them all and buried *Wings of Romance* under Jane Austen in the box for things to keep. Somewhere, still in unpacked boxes in the garage at home, were books she'd given me.

I added the photo albums to the top of the keeping box, thinking I'd go through them later, then started another box with CDs. Her taste in music was similar to her reading – mostly light classics and a lot of Andre Rieu – and I thought most of them could go to Vinnies, checking first that the case contained the CD it stated. Many didn't, and it proved to be a quite a job matching them up.

'Are you okay?' Barbara was framed by the doorway.

'Yep.'

'I thought you'd be finished by now,' said Barbara. 'Maybe you could help me get some of the rubbish into the car and I'll take a load to the tip. There's more than I thought there would be.'

'Are you sure you can manage?' I asked.

'Once I get it into the car, I'll be right. And, anyway, you've got to stay here for the real estate lady, who'll be coming soon.'

I'd almost forgotten. We'd argued about it the night before. I'd told Barbara I wanted her to keep her mouth shut when we met the agent. Our meeting with Richard Law had been a disaster because of her apparent determination to give everything away to this woman claiming to be my daughter. And, since she didn't think she could keep her mouth shut, since she seemed to believe we weren't entitled to all Paloma's things, she said she'd make herself scarce.

As I watched Barbara driving off to the tip, this fiercely independent little woman who was my wife, my eyes filled with tears. Paloma, even in death, was coming between us. Why had she put my name as the father on her daughter's birth certificate?

Back in the unit, I splashed my face with water in the bathroom and dried my eyes, trying to make myself presentable for the agent when she came.

When I emerged from the bathroom, I saw a woman standing in the middle of the living room with her back to me, looking around as if assessing it. But she was wearing jeans with those slashes and treads hanging everywhere, and I thought she should be better dressed than that, when she turned around and faced me.

It was Jenny.

'What are you doing here?' I asked.

'The door was open,' she said.

We still hadn't found the key. We'd better get a locksmith.

I turned the light on. 'How did you know this address?' I was sure I hadn't told her.

'I didn't. I went to your place because I wanted to find out if the DNA kit had arrived, but I saw you and your wife getting into your car, so I followed you.'

'You followed us?' I was yelling again. I seemed to be doing that a lot lately.

'Yes. And I saw you drive down into the car park here, so I just parked out on the street and waited. Then I saw your car again, and it was pretty loaded up, you know, and Barbara was driving, but you weren't in it, so I thought you must still be here somewhere. It had Paloma Grey on the letter box, so I knew what you were doing and I just wanted to see for myself, you know, where she lived. My mother.'

'You've no right to be here.'

'I think I do. She was my mother, after all. There must be stuff here… I'd like to see for myself, that's all. Her things, her stuff. Before you take it all to the tip. Before you destroy everything.'

'I'm sorry, I'll have to ask you to leave.'

'And what if I don't?' She wandered around the room like someone in an art gallery and stood in front of the print of Picasso's *Girl with the Dove* that was still on the wall.

'I might have to call the police.'

'Go on then. I dare you! Some father you turned out to be.'

'I'm not your father.'

'I think you're lying. You probably raped my mother. You just don't want to admit it.'

'No. You're the one who's lying.'

Then the doorbell rang, and, since the door was ajar, the estate agent walked straight in. I don't know how much she overheard, but she was smiling pleasantly and dressed appropriately in a skirt and high heels.

'Okay, I'll be off then,' said Jenny, flipping the hair out of her eyes. 'You'll ring me when you get that kit, won't you?'

'Of course I will.'

As she walked out the door, I turned to the agent and shook her hand.

'Was that your daughter?' she asked.

'No.'

*

Not wanting to worry her, I didn't tell Barbara of Jenny's visit to the unit, and I was very reluctant to leave the unit that night, unlocked. However, I had no choice. Perhaps I was being a bit paranoid or maybe I'd just read too many spy novels, but I put an ornament on the floor, where the hall stand used to be. It would be moved if the door opened wide, and hopefully wouldn't be noticed by the person opening it. There was considerable clutter already on the floor near the door.

It was a little glass pig with wings, that I'd given Paloma when we were young, and I remembered she was a bit miffed, thinking I was implying she was a pig, until I explained about 'pigs might fly' being not so much about the pig, but the flying, that things we think might be impossible could happen. I thought I was being very wise for my age. My father had recently said the same thing to me when I'd announced my plan to study engineering when I left school.

All these memories left me profoundly sad and I was determined to hide this sadness from Barbara, who was lately accusing me of being depressed. She was nagging me about going to the doctor, but I didn't want any happy pills.

The locksmith was coming at ten in the morning, and I persuaded Barbara that I could manage alone at the unit and I'd call her when I had another load ready for the tip or Vinnies.

That morning, I walked with more bounce in my step and smiled as I went about fixing breakfast, and claimed I'd had a great night's sleep when in fact I'd tossed and turned all night, telling myself over and over again that in reality it was unlikely Jenny would return to the unit while it was empty, because she had no way of knowing it was unlocked.

Opening the door a crack, I squeezed in and turned on the light. Everything was exactly as I'd left it. I picked up the flying pig and bubble-wrapped it before adding it to the box of things to keep, which was almost overflowing. I imagined Barbara unwrapping it, frowning at it and asking why on earth I wanted to keep it. Barbara would be furious, of course, claiming we had too much junk anyway.

The locksmith arrived and set about changing the lock, and I got busy with more sorting. Then Barbara rang to let me know the DNA kit had come in the post. She'd already rung Jenny, who wanted to come over that afternoon. From Barbara's cheerful voice on the phone, I gathered Jenny hadn't said anything about the visit to the unit, but I couldn't be sure. Barbara was probably just as good at deceiving me as I was at deceiving her.

Since it was nearly lunchtime by the time the locksmith had finished, I loaded a couple of boxes of items I wanted to keep into the boot of the car and drove home, with one key to the unit on my keyring and the other key in my pocket for the real estate agent. I'd drop that in to her later and sign some documents.

In the garage, I unloaded the two boxes, making space for them by putting some of the old camping gear into a cupboard, and hoping Barbara wouldn't notice that there were two big boxes instead of the one I'd promised. Putting a smile on my face and carrying a couple of photo albums, I climbed the stairs into the living room.

'You were a while,' said Barbara as I entered. 'What on earth were you doing down there?' She would have heard the garage door open, and had probably been timing me! 'Well, I've made sandwiches for lunch.'

'I brought up some photo albums,' I announced, dropping them on the table. 'Thought Jenny might be interested in some photos. Maybe we should go through them first. Just to make sure there's nothing too incriminating.' I smiled broadly to let her know I was joking and prepared to tackle a large sandwich, overflowing with lettuce. 'Hmm, this looks good.'

Sometimes I think you can talk yourself into things. The sandwich was good, despite all that lettuce, and I felt less anxious about the imminent meeting with Jenny.

Jenny came early with a friend, an older woman who took photos of every step in the process. Jenny went first: the mouth swab, putting the scraping into a sterile container, then working up saliva to spit into another small container, then filling out the forms, signing them, attaching bar codes to the containers and forms, then placing them all in the padded envelope provided. It felt funny, when it came to my turn, and I managed to smile for the camera as I was scraping the inside of my cheek and spitting.

There was no mention, in front of Barbara or her friend, of our meeting yesterday, much to my relief. Perhaps she was embarrassed about it. We were both much calmer. With the envelope sealed, she put it into her handbag to be posted. Did I trust her to do that? Doubts nibbled at me.

Barbara stepped up then and announced that we had some photos to show, and she opened the photograph album, starting with the oldest. We squinted at them, because they were small and most were faded.

After we'd turned a few pages, Jenny suddenly said, 'There aren't any of her as a baby. Are you sure this is the first album?'

'As far as I know.' I flipped back a few pages and realised she was right. The album started when she was about four or five years old, about the time she moved in next door. In fact, I was in some of them. We really were like brother and sister in those days.

'I think I know why,' suggested Barbara. 'She had a cleft palate, didn't she? And, well, babies with that aren't exactly…um…beautiful.'

'Yes, that would be right.' I didn't think we needed to say it, but Paloma would have been an ugly baby. 'And she had a lot of surgery, and polio. She would have spent a lot of time in hospital, and she probably wasn't the prettiest little baby, I'm afraid.'

'That's very sad, isn't it?' said Jenny's friend, wrapping a protective arm around Jenny's shoulders.

'Can you inherit a cleft palate?' Jenny asked.

I shrugged.

'It's a birth defect,' said her friend. 'So I suppose it can be genetic.'

'Just as well I couldn't have children then,' said Jenny. 'I have a couple of birth defects too, but they're not obvious. I'm just curious.'

'Of course, dear. You want to know what you might have inherited from your parents. Anyone would.' Barbara really was taking Jenny's side in all this, and I expected she'd be disappointed when she learned I wasn't Jenny's father after all.

There were a couple of photos that Jenny deemed cute, and she asked if she could have them. Barbara – without asking me – took them out of the album and handed them to her. One included me.

The second album proved more interesting. The photos were larger and some were in colour. There was one of Paloma in her early teens standing, holding a pigeon in front of the pigeon loft. I thought I might like to keep that, but Barbara insisted Jenny have it.

'I'll give you a copy,' she said, when she noticed my reluctance to hand it over.

'Do you know Picasso's painting *Child with Dove*?' asked Barbara.

'Yes, there was a print...' Jenny blushed, then glanced at me. 'I mean, I've seen a print of it, somewhere. I don't know where, but, ah...' she cleared her throat, looking at her friend and then back at me, before studying the photo again and smiling. 'It's a lovely picture. Obviously set up to look like the Picasso painting – the way she's holding the bird, and the dress, and the beach ball – except she's a bit older than the girl in the painting, isn't she?'

'Yes,' I said. 'About fourteen or fifteen, I guess.'

'I must get a copy of it,' said Jenny.

'You don't need to,' said Barbara. 'There's one in Paloma's unit. You can have it.'

I had planned to keep that too.

*

Richard Law rang me a few days after this meeting with Jenny. He had received a copy of the original form that Paloma would have filled out following the birth of her daughter, and copies of the adoption papers with her signature. He wanted me to come to his office with samples of my handwriting if possible, when I was about eighteen years old.

'I might be able to find something,' I said, thinking of some of the boxes of stuff I'd been reluctant to throw out which contained my university textbooks, and possibly even some handwritten notes.

'Anything with your signature?' he asked. 'Because signatures change over the years of course.'

'That might be more difficult.' I thought of the Biggles books I'd given Paloma but they were from when I was much younger and I doubted my eighteen-year-old signature was anything like my twelve-year-old signature.

By the next morning, I'd found a few items that might be suitable. *Principles of Structure* – a hefty tome – had my name and address on the inside cover, not exactly a signature, but similar, and there were notes in margins. Barbara found an old aerogram letter I'd written to her a in my early twenties, when she'd travelled to Europe with her family. I was touched that she'd kept it all these years, though the references to missing her sexy arse were a bit embarrassing now. Importantly, it was signed.

*

I opened a good bottle of French bubbles after our meeting with Richard Law. The alleged 'father's signature' on the form that had been filled out before the issuing of Jenny's birth certificate was not mine. I had doubts too about Paloma's signature on that form.

Barbara was disappointed, but she managed to cheer up after a couple of glasses of wine. I decided to ring George and tell him the news.

'It happens more often than you might think,' said George. 'And of course, it's a criminal offence to falsify a record like that.'

'She must have been very desperate,' I said, 'to do something like that.' I imagined her in her hospital bed, filling out the forms – as Barbara and I had done when our own children were born – but for Paloma it wouldn't have been a happy event. There would have been tears; she would have been pressured into giving the baby up for adoption.

'I don't know what you're planning to do about Jenny,' said George, 'but perhaps you should wait for the DNA results before telling her.'

'That's what Richard recommended,' I said. 'The results will go to her address and mine, so we should both receive them at much the same time.'

'Good.' George was silent for a moment. 'Do you have any idea why Paloma did this?'

'I think because she loved me – or thought she did.'

'Yes, I'm sure she did,' said George.

'I wonder who the father really was. Do you have any ideas? Maybe it's true that she was raped.' I suspected he knew more about Paloma than he was prepared to say. He'd known her for a long time. If she trusted him with her will, she might have trusted him with her secrets.

'Sorry, no. Thank you for letting me know,' he said, now seemingly in a hurry to get off the phone.

'That's okay. I'll call again when we get the DNA results.'

At a little after three in the morning, I woke in a sweat with terrible indigestion, and regretted the champagne and the bottle of red we'd shared – though I'd had more than half of both.

After going to the toilet, I lay back in bed beside Barbara, who was sleeping soundly. I felt profoundly sad, watching her soft breathing and eyes fluttering under eyelids as she dreamed. What about? We can never know or understand another person completely. I loved Barbara, this tiny woman with her huge heart, who was willing to accept Jenny, believing she was possibly my daughter by another woman, into her life. She was actually disappointed when the truth was revealed. I felt so much in love I felt my heart would burst and I started crying. I didn't deserve Barbara's love. Tears were running down my cheeks onto my pillow and, fearing I'd wake her, I got out of bed.

I found myself in the garage, rummaging through the boxes of books I'd collected from Paloma's place. I looked again at my message and signature on *Wings of Romance* and saw that it was similar – almost identical – to the signature on the forms Paloma had filled out after Jenny was born. So she'd copied my twelve-year-old signature!

I lifted another box of books down from the top of a cupboard. It was heavy and strained my chest and arm, but I got it down onto the floor and opened it. Pain throbbed down my left arm and my indigestion was getting worse, but I didn't heed the warning. I was too concerned now to go through these books that I'd saved for our grandchildren and found a big colourful book called *Mechanical Projects*, a sort of do-it-yourself book for budding engineers, that Paloma had given me for my thirteenth birthday. She'd signed it, with love. Her signature was very neat. The P in Paloma was about twice the height of the other letters and fairly upright, as was the G in Grey, and the tail of the y stopped abruptly after a delicate curl.

I took the books upstairs to my study because I wanted to see again my copy of Paloma's will and a thank you card she'd sent to us after Toby's burial. The more recent signatures were quite different. The loop on her P was much larger, towering over the dwarfed remaining letters, and leaning in on them, like a tree in a stiff breeze. Her G was similarly large compared with the other letters, and the tail on the final y had grown into a sweeping underline of her whole signature.

I suddenly felt very ill. I can remember crashing into the desk where I'd put the books, and feeling as if an elephant was sitting on my chest. It was hard to breathe and I realised I was in trouble. Then Barbara was leaning over me, and I was telling her I was sorry. Again.

I can't remember the ambulance. The next few hours or days are a jumble. I thought I saw cockroaches coming out of the air conditioning vent in intensive care. Worried one might drop into my open mouth, I tried to warn the nurses, but I couldn't make a sound. Everyone seemed to ignore me. They just went about their business, sticking things into my arms, chest, down my throat. I realise now that much of what I saw or thought I saw was hallucination or a dream. It's hard to know the difference.

I was running through a bamboo forest. It was so hard to breathe. Then I saw Barbara and she was wearing her bamboo tent, a dress she wore when she was pregnant with our boys. It was green, to match her eyes – only Barbara didn't have green eyes. I kept seeing Paloma's eyes on Barbara's face. It was the drugs, I suppose. Everything was green. The doctors and nurses all wore green. Someone told me to count backwards from ten. I got to eight.

Things gradually came together when I was back in the ward. Back from where, though? I thought it might be Barbara sitting beside me. Someone was talking to me, inside my head, saying, 'I don't think I'll ever forgive him for what he did to Paloma.' Who said that? It wasn't Barbara, but it was so real. It wasn't a dream.

I woke in a sweat. Barbara was there, with her own eyes, not Paloma's, and she was swimming a bit until she wiped my eyes with a tissue and I could see clearly. The cockroaches had gone. I was in a different room with bamboo-patterned curtains.

Barbara was smiling. She leant over and kissed me.

I tried to speak. 'How…' It came out croaky.

She gave me some ice to suck. My throat was sore.

'How long have you been here?' I asked.

'A while,' she said. 'The boys are at home. They flew in yesterday.'

'Is it Christmas again?'

'No, silly. They came because they were worried about you. I've got to ring them, let them know you're awake.'

'I'm all right, I think. What happened?'

I must have nodded off again as she was telling me. The gist of it was that I'd had a heart attack. They'd done an angiogram (I don't remember that), then sent me to intensive care… And that's when I faded out.

When I woke again, she'd gone. My chest hurt and when I slipped my hand under my gown and rubbed it I could feel rough lumps under my skin.

'Don't touch that,' said a nurse who came to fiddle with the machine beside me.

'What's happening?' I asked.

'Everything's going well,' she said. 'You've had a big operation. A triple bypass.'

'Heart?'

'Yes.'

'I don't remember.'

'Probably just as well.' She went on to explain about the various tubes draining my body and the tube that was delivering drugs and fluid, and that if I needed anything I was to press the red buzzer. She put it in my hand.

I closed my eyes. *I'll never forgive him for what he did to Paloma.* Of course it was Mrs Grey – Paloma's mother. I'd come home with my washing. Mrs Grey was talking to my mother in the living room, and, not wanting to get involved, I went around the back to the laundry to put on the machine. I waited there until I heard the front door close, and Mrs Grey's footsteps on the path.

When I opened my eyes again, Barbara was beside my bed with our two boys. They were all smiling. On a shelf on the wall opposite the bed there were blue irises in a vase and an elaborate bouquet of Australian native flowers.

We must have taught our sons to tackle drama with humour and my sons were full of infarct and fart jokes, and awful urine/you're-out puns. It hurt to laugh.

Mr Grey, Paloma's father, had green eyes. *I'll never forgive him for what he did to Paloma.* I'd assumed Mrs Grey was talking about me. I'd thought it was because I'd neglected Paloma when it was so obvious she needed someone to talk to. She needed a friend and I couldn't be bothered.

Something terrible had happened. Mr Grey had left. He'd gone when I had my eighteenth birthday party. Was it because of what happened? Is that why Paloma got so drunk that night?

I closed my eyes again, seeing Paloma in her big baggy nightie in the laundry that night, with her bare feet covered in damp grass clippings. She'd put on weight. I tried to remember any other time I'd seen her that year, perhaps over the fence, somewhere in the garden. That choko vine had grown like a jungle over the fence and pigeon loft. No one was maintaining their garden, and then the pigeon loft was emptied. I can remember my mother saying something about that. She was relieved. I could now hang my washing out on the clothes line overnight and it wouldn't be covered in bird shit in the morning.

I was sitting up in bed after breakfast and my first shower, when Barbara brought Jenny in to see me.

'We've got the DNA results,' Barbara said, leaning over to give me a kiss, then putting a protective arm around Jenny's waist.

'Oh. I'd forgotten about that.'

'It's complicated,' said Jenny. 'Didn't make much sense at first. I had to ring them so they could explain.'

Barbara sat on the bed next to me, and Jenny sat in the chair, looking down at the floor.

'I'm sorry, I really thought you were my father, but you're not. I really wanted you to be him.' She flashed me a shy smile. 'The truth is not nice, though.' She looked to Barbara for help and took a deep shuddering breath, like someone who had been crying.

Barbara reached out and held her hand. 'It seems Jenny is the result of an incestuous relationship. They sometimes discover this with DNA tests.'

'Oh.' I didn't know what to say.

'It explains a few things, though,' said Jenny. 'I couldn't have children because of some sort of genetic defect, and that was one reason I was so keen to find my birth parents. It's a bit scary, though. Recessive genes are more likely to be passed on when the parents are related. Like my eye colour.'

'Paloma's father had your eye colour.'

'I thought he might.' Jenny looked down at the floor again, then looked up at me. 'My ex wanted children and when I couldn't give them to him, he went and found someone who could.' She shrugged. 'But I guess it's just as well. I should be glad there's not more wrong with me. I mean I could have been a bit, you know, retarded or something. I'm lucky really that I was adopted by my parents.'

I said. 'So do you think your father might have been Paloma's father?'

'My grandfather. Yes, it makes sense.'

'It does. I've been thinking about something that happened when I was about eighteen. The last few days I kept hearing this voice in my head – maybe it was the drugs, I don't know – but it was as clear as yesterday. Someone said *I don't think I can ever forgive him for what he did to Paloma.* I remembered then that it was Paloma's mother, talking to my mother. She was what you'd call a control freak when it came to Paloma. I overheard it. They probably didn't know I was in earshot. My mother didn't like Mrs Grey very much either because usually when she came to visit it was to complain about something I'd done.'

'What was ah, my grandfather like?'

I shrugged. 'He was a soldier. He'd won medals, and he used to show them to Paloma and me. He had a lot of stories about what he did during the war. I liked him when I was a kid. And Paloma adored him.'

Barbara handed me a tissue, and I wiped my eyes.

It was a moment before I could speak again. 'What a monster. What an awful breach of trust.'

'No wonder her mother would never forgive him,' said Barbara.

I nodded. 'That year, the year you were born, Jenny, I was pretty self-absorbed. I knew something was wrong, but I didn't want to know about it. Poor Paloma. I'd abandoned her.'

Jenny, the girl who wasn't my daughter, hugged me as I broke down and cried on her shoulder.

We were interrupted by a nurse who came to check on me, as my heart, which was being monitored, seemed to be beating very fast.

'You know what I think,' I said, after the nurse had finished fussing, 'I don't think Paloma knew she had a daughter. She couldn't have kept a secret like that all her life. And, if she did know, I'm sure she would have wanted to find you. I think it was her mother…'

I was imagining Paloma in hospital, coming out of an anaesthetic after a caesarean. You get confused. You're not sure what's real.

'I just can't imagine Paloma willingly handing her daughter over for adoption,' I said. 'She didn't know. Perhaps she believed the baby had died. I bet her mother organised everything. After all, Paloma was only just eighteen. And her mother would have taken over. She would have filled out those forms, and she would have lied about the father, of course.'

Barbara was nodding. 'It makes sense. Even though I didn't know her for very long, I could see that Paloma was a very brave and determined woman. You're right, John. There's no way she'd give Jenny away without a fight.'

'I'm sorry you never met your mother,' I said, putting my arms around Jenny and giving her a hug. 'I bet Mrs Grey put my name down on those forms. I mean, who else was she going to put? Not the real father, of course – the man she could never forgive.'

Jenny added, 'Of course, no one's going to put the real father down when it's incest. I don't think anyone would have adopted me if they thought I might have genetic problems.'

'And she wouldn't expect anyone to ever go searching for them,' said Barbara. 'John, I showed those papers to Jenny, and explained that it wasn't your signature. They were on your desk when you collapsed, along with some children's books. You must have been looking for something.'

'Yes, I was. Mrs Grey copied my twelve-year-old signature from a book I'd given Paloma.' I laughed. 'But it was nothing like my eighteen-year-old one.'

*

Armed with a bunch of roses and a bottle of bubbly, Barbara and I are standing outside Paloma's unit, now owned by her daughter, Jenny, who has invited us over for lunch. Since Paloma's will gave us the freedom to do what we wanted with her bequest, and there was no doubt Jenny was Paloma's daughter, we organised for the unit to be transferred to her.

She's adopted us. Calls us Uncle John and Aunty Barbara and gives us both a hug before finding a vase for the roses. When she gets to meet the rest of the family, she plans to adopt them too, and I think that's a good idea.

It's the first time I've seen the unit since my trip to hospital. I'm surprised. The walls are off-white, the new carpet is pale blue. Glass doors leading out to the courtyard are open and sunlight streams into the living area. Jenny has constructed a terraced garden with wooden sleepers and planted orange marigolds, yellow daisies and bright red geraniums.

I can't help remembering our lunch with Paloma in this dreary unit and that poor stupid dog she loved so much. The print of Picasso's *Child with a Dove* is exactly where it used to be, on the wall opposite the dining table, above the sideboard, which has been moved from the living area. Directly under it is an enlarged framed photo of Paloma holding a pigeon in a similar dress and pose.

There is no dining table, and I wonder where we are going to sit to eat lunch. I still feel Paloma's presence in this room, perhaps watching us through the eyes of the photo. She'd be pleased to see her daughter here.

I hope Paloma can see that I'm trying to make amends for all the times I was too busy to listen, too caught up with my own grand schemes, too self-important to notice, to even notice that she was pregnant.

And here she is putting the vase with the roses on the sideboard. 'I thought we'd eat outside, since the weather's so nice,' says Jenny, not Paloma. 'Have a look around while I get some glasses.'

Sitting on the sideboard, with their backs against the wall, are two rag dolls I thought I'd thrown out. I'm curious about how they'd made their way back.

'Just as well we didn't throw them out,' says Barbara, answering my unasked question. 'Undress them and you'll see.'

The boy doll wears a blue and white gingham shirt, and dark blue baggy pants held up with braces. The girl doll wears a matching gingham pinafore, over a dress that matches the boy's pants. When I remove their clothes, I see their names written on their pale cotton skin: Paloma Grey and John Higgins.

'They were filthy,' Barbara explains, 'so I thought I'd give them a wash.'

'Aren't they cute?' says Jenny. 'And look, this one, the girl, has green eyes. But the boy's eyes are brown like yours.'

I nod, a lump in my throat preventing me from speaking, so I dress the dolls and put them back on the sideboard.

'I thought you might like to give them to your grandchildren,' says Jenny.

'Oh, they've got enough toys,' says Barbara. 'And I don't think they'd appreciate them as much as you do.'

We wander outside, where Jenny has placed an ice bucket and three glasses on a small mosaic table.

I pop the champagne cork. 'To Paloma,' I say, as we clink our glasses.

Stinky Creek

At my father's funeral, my brother, Greg, spoke about our 'legendary' camping trip to Stinky Creek. I couldn't believe what I was hearing. We never went there; it was where Dad always threatened to take us if we were naughty. It was supposed to be horrible, and as a small child I lived in fear of the place, but as I grew older I realised it never existed.

But there was Greg, standing in front of all Dad's old friends, telling them about the fun we had erecting the tent, building the camp fire, cooking bacon and eggs for breakfast, and the fish we caught.

Later, at the wake, while pouring endless cups of tea and handing out tons of lamingtons to Dad's nursing home 'family', I confronted my brother about Stinky Creek. 'I'm so embarrassed,' I told him. 'How could you stand up there and talk about a place that doesn't exist!'

'Stinky Creek?' he asked.

Old Mr Bennet, who was standing nearby, overheard us. 'Oh, your father was always talking about Stinky Creek. I'm so glad you mentioned that. It was his favourite place.'

Dad had been suffering from dementia for some years and he often spoke rubbish – we knew it was rubbish. He'd always been a good storyteller, and the stories he told were often credible as he filled in the memory blanks with what might have happened, stitching things together to make sense of the world he no longer understood.

Greg studied me with his head cocked at an angle. 'You really don't remember it?' he asked.

'Oh, I remember the threats, but…'

'Don't you remember how we thought we were so clever pitching the tent under a big gum tree, and Dad coming along and telling us to pull it down because a branch might fall on us. So we re-erected it closer to the creek. Mind you, Dad was busy fishing all this time. Then he came and inspected our work and told us to pull it down again, and move it further away from the creek, because if it rained overnight and the creek flooded, we'd all be drowned'

'Sure, I remember Dad telling us about branches falling from trees and killing people sleeping inside tents, and the creek flooding and drowning people. He just said those things to frighten us. We never went there.'

'We did.'

'Didn't.'

'Did.'

Now we were squabbling like children. I put my hands over my ears and returned to the kitchen, where I had hidden a small bottle of whisky. With no one looking, I took a swig, refilled the teapot and returned to the dining room, where tea-deprived ancients were waiting with empty cups.

Greg was talking to a group of women and they were all laughing. As wakes go, this was a fairly cheerful affair. We had lost Dad slowly as his mind slipped away before his body, and in his last weeks he rarely recognised anyone and preferred the landscape behind his closed eyes even when awake. That's when I cried. Now that his body had been reduced to ashes, it seemed like a cause for celebration. The end of an era.

I poured tea into Mr Bennet's cup and waited while he helped himself to milk and sugar from the tray on the sideboard.

'What are you going to do with the ashes, dear?' he asked.

I shrugged. I hadn't thought about it.

'What about scattering them at Stinky Creek?' he suggested.

'Good idea.' I forced a smile onto my lips as I moved around the room with the teapot, Mr Bennet trailing behind. I finished up beside Greg.

'Your sister told me she's going to scatter your dad's ashes at Stinky Creek,' he told Greg and the gaggle of women nearby.

I bit my lip.

'What a good idea,' said Greg. 'Let's do that. He'd love it.'

*

Dad's ashes were on the back seat, Greg was at the wheel and I was in the passenger seat. We'd left our families at home as we made this brother-and-sister journey to Stinky Creek. It's not on any map, but Greg insisted he knew exactly where it was. Since driving through Tamworth, I'd lost my sense of direction.

He turned off the bitumen road onto a dirt track. 'Don't you remember this?' he asked.

Dust billowed around us and I wound up the window. 'No. It all looks very dry. I can't imagine there'd be a creek anywhere near here.'

'Oh, there is. You just wait.'

'Why is it called Stinky Creek?' I asked, bracing myself as we bumped over the potholes.

'I think it's named after someone called Mr Stinky.'

'Sounds like a character from a children's book. I always believed it was because of the bad smell. I'm sure Dad told us there was a terrible smell.'

Greg swerved the car to the left and right and branches scraped the roof. I was glad it was his car, not mine.

'That's what he told us,' Greg said, 'but you know Dad. He had a tendency to exaggerate. There is a smell, but it's not unpleasant.'

The road dipped then veered to the left and Greg stopped the car in front of a large boulder. 'We're here.'

I stared at the boulder that blocked our way.

'We have to get out and walk,' Greg explained. 'It's not far.'

I opened the door and breathed in the tang of eucalypt and squelch of mud – distinctive but not unpleasant.

'I'll carry the ashes, will I?' Greg was so organised he'd even bought a backpack for the urn.

'Shall I carry the water, then?' I asked, reaching for the bottle we'd shared during the drive.

'Won't need it,' said Greg. 'It's a spring-fed creek and the water's good.'

We climbed around the boulder and found ourselves in another world of trees, soft grasses and a babbling creek running over smooth pebbles. We followed it a little way until it dropped into a deep pond filled with sparkling water. Of course! I remembered this place. We'd pitched our tent under that gum tree the first time we came here with Dad.

Greg and I stood on the bank above the pond and we stared at our reflected selves. Greg unplugged the urn, and together we shook out the fine ash which fell gently onto the water's surface, because there was no breeze. We were watched by a kookaburra family who immediately started up their cackle as if sharing our joy.

*

'I'm sorry,' I say to my husband and children as we leave the doctor's consulting room.

They are all crying, but I think I've known this for a while now. It's more than just forgetting where I put my keys.

'Don't be sorry, darling.' My husband puts his arm around me. 'You can't help it. It's hereditary.'

'But I don't know what will happen.' I'm anxious, already trying to understand what just happened, trying to remember. For a while, I thought I was back at school, doing exams. I was a good student then.

'Don't worry, Mum,' says my daughter. 'We'll look after you.'

'I might live for a long time,' I say, as I try and imagine the future.

My poor daughter smiles through her tears, trying to comfort me, telling me not to worry.

But I can't help worrying. I'm going to slip away as my father did, brain before body. My family will make excuses for me, for the strange things I do and say, until it gets worse. Then they'll form a circle around me as I'm sitting on one of those recliner seats like Dad, and they'll be telling me their names, and I won't remember who they are. They'll wait patiently, hoping for a glimmer of recognition.

In the car on the way home, I talk about the happy times I can remember, the things we did as a family when the girls were young.

'Remember when we went camping at Stinky Creek?' I begin.

'Mum, there's no such place as Stinky Creek. When we were little, you used to threaten to take us camping there when we were naughty. And you told us scary stories about people being killed when branches fell on their tents, and how the water rises when it rains and about getting swept down the creek.'

My other daughter laughs. 'We never believed it, Mum.' She squeezes my hand to reassure me. 'And remember the pond? It was an evil place with mud that sucked you down and monsters lurking just below the surface.'

I nod. The monsters. I'd forgotten about the monsters lurking just below the surface. I can feel myself being sucked down, down, down into that stinking mud. I can't fight it.

Déjà vu

As soon as she entered the Riverview Boutique Hotel, Monique felt she'd been here before. But how? Her home was in Brantome, a French village and she was now in Kyogle, a town in northern New South Wales. She'd never been to Australia before; she'd lived in Brantome for fifty years, where she'd owned a nursery and flower shop until she sold it six weeks ago; she'd never travelled more than a few kilometres from her village, never been to Paris until two days ago. Only two days? It seemed longer. Perhaps it was jet lag. Perhaps she was dreaming.

When Monique had accepted an offer for her business, she retired, thinking it would be nice to have time to sit in her own garden, smell the lavender and lilac in the evenings, spend her mornings walking along the River Dronne, visit the cafés and have more time with her friends, especially her close friend Jane, who had recently retired from the school where she taught English. Jane had her family, though. Invariably, when Monique rang to see if she would like to go for walk or a horse ride, she'd find Jane occupied with her family. Monique's little cottage now seemed very empty.

Then, a month ago, a letter arrived from Australia. Ralph Woods had written to inform her of the death of his father, Jack. He had apparently found her name and address amongst his father's belongings.

Monique examined the brief letter and its envelope. The writer had not provided her with a return address. She showed it to Jane, who deciphered the postmark: Kyogle, Australia.

'Who do you know in Australia?' she asked.

Monique shrugged.

That night she dreamed of her brother, whom she hadn't seen since she was a child. She hadn't thought of him for almost forty years, when he'd left home, and she woke as if from a nightmare. Was Ralph Woods the son of Jacques Desbois, her brother?

In the morning, she visited Jane, who found Kyogle on her computer. Together they translated the website into English.

'You know, I'd like to go there,' said Monique. 'It looks nice, with a river and forests, and I might have family there. If I have got family, then…' She didn't want to explain how alone she felt. Instead she smiled. 'It would be nice, wouldn't it, if I had a nephew? Maybe he's married, maybe he has children. It doesn't say.' She held up the letter again and scrutinised it as if it might have some coded message. 'Would you help me? I'll need a passport, won't I? And I'll have to go by plane. I'm frightened of flying. I've never done anything like this before. Maybe now is the time.'

*

The Riverview's owner was Susan Granger, and Monique had never seen her before. She was a robust but attractive blonde woman with freckles, and Monique thought she looked like a tennis player or maybe a swimmer. Australians are very athletic.

'You must be exhausted,' Susan said, picking up the suitcase. 'I'll show you to your room.'

'Certainly, I am.' Monique followed her up the stairs. 'I've been travelling for two days. I'm hoping to find a man here called Ralph Woods. Do you know him?'

'No, I don't think so.' She unlocked the door. 'There's no smoking in the rooms, but there's a balcony and I've provided an ashtray on the little table out there. I hope you'll be comfortable.'

'Oh yes,' said Monique, touching the back of the upholstered chair, the quilt and pillows on the bed. 'Everything just feels like home. I don't know how that can be, when I'm so far away. It feels very strange, like I'm in some sort of dream.'

'Now, what was the name of that person you wanted to contact?'

'Ralph Woods. He wrote me a letter to tell me his father had died.'

'I'll give it some thought. If there's anything else you need, just let me know.' She closed the door behind her.

*

Susan Granger watched from the kitchen door as her guest, Monique, nibbled at her croissant. Susan's breakfasts were legendary in Kyogle: two eggs, bacon, sausages, a slab of toast and butter she churned herself, and all this woman wanted was a croissant! She shrugged, reminding herself that the customer is always right, and continued stacking the dishwasher. Since starting up her little hotel two years ago, she'd had no trouble with guests.

One of her regulars, Eric, was down by the river with his easel, painting the morning mist. He'd arrived last night and, after sharing a bottle of wine with her, he'd asked her if she'd pose for him, nude. Last year he'd painted her, fully clothed, reading under a willow tree, and she'd admired the painting so he gave it to her. She felt obliged then to deduct some money from his tariff, and had hung the painting in the dining room.

While they drank wine last night, he sketched her face, telling her how much he admired her bone structure. She didn't know him well, except that he was some sort of doctor who held a clinic in the local medical centre a few times a year. That probably meant he was harmless, so she said she'd think about posing nude.

Susan picked up the coffee pot and took it to Monique, who had finished her croissant.

'I had a thought about Ralph Woods. There's a chap called Ralph does some odd jobs around here. I don't know what his surname is, but I'll ask around for you.'

'*Merci.*'

Susan poured the coffee. 'Did you sleep well?'

'*Non.* I am, how do you say, too upset…*non*, disturbed, *oui*? I feel

I'm at home, but I'm not. It's impossible to be here on the other side of the world. I have dreams, and when I wake I'm not sure if they're dreams or not. This place, does it have ghosts?'

'Not that I know of. Mind you, I've only been here two years. You're probably suffering some jet lag. I know it can be difficult to settle after you've travelled so far, and your body rhythms get out of whack.'

'What does that mean? Out of whack?'

'Like you can't set your body clock.'

'Ah, I understand. But you know the worst thing about travelling in a plane?'

'What?'

'You cannot smoke. I think when I get here that I will give up smoking, I've been so long without a cigarette. I'm tearing my hair. My friend says I should give up smoking, it's not good for me. But when I finish my coffee, I will go upstairs and use the ashtray you have so thoughtfully provided.'

'Your friend who made the booking said in her email that you enjoyed smoking and asked if I had a smoking room.'

'She is a good friend. I don't know about computers and emails, so she helps me with everything like that.'

'Have you had enough to eat?' Susan asked, as Monique rose from the table.

'*Oui. Merci.* I don't have much hunger.' She stood in front of a watercolour above the fireplace. 'Do you know who painted this?' she asked. 'Because I know this place. I have been here before. I remember this willow tree. We used to play under it when we were children.'

'It was painted just down the river a little way. It was a present from an artist friend. He's here now, near the river somewhere.'

'I don't know. I can't explain it, but I will go and look at that willow tree soon.'

*

Eric was doing another painting of the willow when he suddenly noticed a thin dark-haired woman standing under it, as if she had risen from the mist, which swirled around her. Quickly, before she moved, he dabbed some dark on his canvas – he would add detail later. She stood exactly where Susan had sat reading in last year's painting. Susan had been a blob of light, shining through the deep shadows cast by the willow in the midday sun.

This dark woman was a shadow in the sunlit cavern formed by the willow, the sun now just cresting the nearby hills. Behind the willow, beneath the mist, the river was still and silent, and on the other side of the river was a forest of hoop pine. Whipbirds greeted the morning with their shrill cry.

She hadn't noticed him. Choosing a finer brush, he lightened her face, in profile under thick black hair; then he worked on her posture, which was stiff, hands out in front as though fending off an attacker. He wondered if perhaps she was an actress, rehearsing a role, because there was nothing he could see that might cause her to be frightened.

He felt like a voyeur, spying on some very private moment, so he decided to announce his presence. 'Watch out for the drop bears,' he called.

She jumped. '*Quoi?*'

'Drop bears,' he said, '*Thylarctus plummetus.*' And when she still didn't get it he translated into French: '*koala deposer*' raising his hands, and dropping them. 'They fall out of the trees – *ils tombent.*'

She came out from under the willow, wrapping her arms around herself as if cold, and walked towards him. 'Oh, I'm sorry I didn't know about the drop bears.'

'It's okay,' he laughed. 'It's an Australian joke.'

'They don't exist?'

'No. *Non.*'

'But you are a painter, *un artiste?*'

'*Oui,*' he answered, moving aside so she could see what he had done.

'*Parlez-vous Français?*' she asked.

'*Un peu,*' he said. 'I studied in France as a young man, but since that was some time ago, I'm very rusty.'

She inspected his painting and praised it, and after a while he persuaded her to take up her position again under the willow tree. He asked her to raise her hands while he caught the light on her fingers.

They chatted and she told him that there used to be a willow tree just like this in her home town that had been uprooted during a flood. The painting in the dining room had reminded her of it.

'When I first saw you,' he said, 'you looked as if you'd had a very bad fright, or maybe…'

'Oh, I don't know. It was nothing.' She shrugged and laughed, but the fear was still in her eyes. She jumped as a whipbird shrilled from somewhere on the other side of the river. 'What is that? I thought it might be a drop bear!' She laughed. 'But it's some sort of bird, yes?'

'A whipbird. It's probably tearing strips of bark from the trunks looking for breakfast. When it finds something good to eat, he calls his mate so they can share their feast. Speaking of which, I haven't had breakfast yet.' He balanced his painting against his knee while he folded his easel and packed his paints into a large bag.

'Can I carry something?' she asked.

Eric gave her the painting, which wasn't dry enough to put into the bag. 'Why have you come to Kyogle?' he asked.

'It's probably silly, now I think about it, now I'm here. I have lived all my life in a little village in France, and this is a very big trip for me, so I'm nervous, I suppose, jumpy – and when you tell me about drop bears, I get upset.'

'I'm sorry. You looked frightened before I mentioned the drop bears, though.'

'I think I was remembering something about the willow tree in Brantome, but *ça ne fait rien,* it doesn't matter. I have come here because I want to find someone called Ralph Woods, who might be my nephew, my brother's son. But maybe I'm on a wild goose chase.'

They walked together towards the hotel.

'So did you study art when you were in France?' she asked, after a while.

Eric laughed. 'No. I wish! I studied psychiatry.'

'So you are a head shrink? You must think you have met a mad woman.'

'No, you're not mad. Maybe a bit anxious and frightened, though. As you say, it's a big trip and you're in a strange country, in a town that must be very different.'

'*Non*. That's the problem. It's very similar here. Everything feels like home. I can't explain it.'

'*Déjà vu?*'

'*Oui.*'

*

'Who?' Ralph asked Susan Granger, who was on the other end of the phone. 'Mademoiselle Who?'

'Monique Desbois. She's a guest in my hotel and she's hoping to meet you.'

The name sounded familiar, but Ralph couldn't place it.

'She's come from France. Made the booking a couple of weeks ago.'

'I have no idea who she is,' Ralph admitted, 'but if you want to give her my mobile number, that's okay.'

'I'll do that, then. And she can explain.'

*

That afternoon, while he was mending Mrs Moore's front gate that had come off its hinges, Ralph received a call from Mademoiselle Monique Desbois.

'Did you write to me to tell me of your father's death?' she asked. 'You didn't put an address on the envelope, so I can't be sure.'

'I don't think so,' he said. 'I'm not much of a letter writer. What did I...'

The penny dropped. He'd written to a few of the people named in his father's old address book. So she was one of his father's women. His heart sank. And she'd come all the way from France. How could he get rid of her?

'Was your father's name Jacques?'

'Sorry, lady, no, it was Jack. Jack Woods.'

'Jack,' she repeated.

There was silence.

'Hello?' he asked after he felt she'd had enough time to process the fact that she'd come all this way for no reason. 'Are you still there?'

'*Oui*. Yes. But you did write to me, did you not, to tell me of his death? You said you found my name with his things.'

'Look, lady, I don't know who you are or what you want, but my dad died penniless. He had a lot of lady friends too, so I don't want to disappoint you but there's nothing here for you.'

'Oh, but you don't understand,' she said. 'I'm not one of your father's lady friends. I am perhaps his sister.'

Ralph laughed. 'No way. He didn't have any family.'

'Perhaps I'm not. Perhaps I have made a mistake,' she said, 'but I wonder if we could meet and I can explain. I have brought some photos of my brother and if I could show them to you we may know for certain.'

'Lady, I didn't have much to do with my old man. We didn't get on.'

'What can be the harm?' she asked. 'I have come a long way, and I'm hoping you might be my nephew. But if you're not, it doesn't matter. I'm curious to know. That is all.'

*

While he waited in a booth at the Paragon Milk Bar, Ralph remembered seeing his father just before his death. He hadn't recognised this man who'd spent the last four years of his life in Grafton Correctional Centre. When Jack had become ill and was hospitalised, the authorities had informed Ralph and his sister, as the next of kin, that their father had cancer of the liver; he was dying. Ralph volunteered to drive to the coast. His father was in palliative care, did not recognise him, and had nothing to say. Ralph did, however, become friendly with a nurse, and took her out to dinner.

Then he received a phone call from the nurse to tell him his father had passed away. Poor girl was crying, seemed really upset about it. She told him he'd have to organise a funeral and that there was a box of his father's possessions to be collected.

There wasn't much in the box, certainly nothing of any value. However, there was an old address book and a few sepia photos, which at the time had meant nothing to Ralph. He'd brought them to this meeting with Monique in the Paragon Milk Bar, and had taken them out of their envelope.

He rehearsed how he would try to explain things to Monique. In one version, he would tell the truth: his father was a sex offender, and they finally caught him, locked him up for what he'd done to all those young women, and some young girls. In the other version, he would claim no knowledge of his father's life, because he'd left when they were children. That much was true. With the first version, he wasn't sure how much he would say. Would he tell Monique about what had happened to his little sister? If he lied, how would he be able to explain finding Monique's address and the letter he wrote?

It would depend on who Monique was. He didn't want to upset her too much.

'So, this is the Paragon?'

He was startled by the tall dark-haired woman standing beside the booth.

'I had expected something a bit grander.'

He stood, and gestured for her to sit opposite him. 'Hi, I'm Ralph.' He shook her hand across the table. 'Can I get you something? A coffee? They have a cappuccino machine here.'

'*Non*, I'll have a milk shake please. *Chocolat*. My friend Eric who drove me here says I must have a milk shake. And you? Will you have a glass of wine or a beer?'

'No, I'll have a milk shake too. They don't sell alcohol in milk bars. You have to go to the pub for beer or wine.'

'You must think I'm a fool. Are they your photos?'

'Yes. Not much, I'm afraid, and they're very small and hard to see. But have a squiz and I'll get our drinks.'

'*Merci*.' She grabbed them and flipped through them.

When he returned to the booth, she pushed one of the photos towards him. 'See that. I have that same photo. It's me on that horse with my brother, Jacques. We called her Nefertiti.' She opened her handbag and drew out an envelope of similar sepia photos. 'Like you, I don't have many and they are tiny, but see. It is the same, *oui*?'

'Well, I'll be a monkey's uncle.'

She looked confused, then laughed. 'Oh, it's another Australian joke, *non*? The monkey's uncle. Because I think I am your aunt, and this is not an Australian joke, or a French joke either.' She looked very earnest, and he saw tears welling in her eyes.

Their milkshakes arrived, and he still didn't know what he was going to tell her about his father. They sucked their straws in silence.

'Look, this isn't easy for me,' he said after a while. 'I didn't know he had any family, but this could be him, I think.' He flipped through the photos in her envelope. '…and if we both have the same photo… I guess it must be him.' He returned them to the envelope and handed them back. 'I'm not sure how to say this, but Dad wasn't a very nice person. I know you've come a long way and,' he paused, 'you probably should know the truth.'

'I must know the truth,' she said. 'It's difficult for me too, because I can't remember much. It's a long time ago, and every time I try to think about it, I get a terrible feeling, like a bad fright…do you know the words *déjà vu*? It's like everything that's happening now has happened before, like I've been here before, but it makes no sense. I told Eric about this feeling – he's staying in the same hotel, and I met him this morning – he says it might be a repressed memory, something from the past that I can't quite remember. You must tell me the truth. Why do you say my brother was not a nice person?'

Ralph shook his head. He didn't have much time for this sort of hocus pocus. 'Okay, you asked for it,' he said. 'He was a sex offender.' He kept his eyes on the formica table top, unable to meet hers. 'He raped little girls and he raped my little sister. My mother threw him out of the house, and I don't know what he's done with most of his life, but I can guess. They caught him at it – the police caught him doing it to a kid…' He couldn't continue, anger choked his words. He looked up.

Her eyes were wide, her hand over her mouth as if she might be sick.

He reached across the table, touched her lightly on the arm. 'I'm sorry,' he said. 'Are you okay?'

She nodded, but she didn't look it.

*

Susan Granger helped Monique to her room. The woman looked as if she had seen a ghost and couldn't stop shivering. Ralph Woods had driven her home, saying something about a shock, and then claiming he had to run because he was late for a job.

'I'm needing a cigarette and then I'll be all right,' Monique said, as she pulled a pack from her purse and opened the doors to the balcony. Her hands trembled as she tried to hold the lighter to the end of her cigarette.

Susan stood in the doorway unsure about leaving her alone. 'Can I get you anything?' she asked. 'Perhaps a doctor?'

'*Non, non*, I don't need a doctor.' She inhaled deeply and blew the smoke through her nose. 'See, I feel better already. It's just my addiction to cigarettes that's the trouble. I'll give them up soon.'

'Perhaps you'd like something to drink?'

'*Oui*, something stronger than a chocolate milkshake would be nice.'

'We have some very good Australian wine. Perhaps a pinot noir?'

'*Merci*. Thank you.'

She did appear calmer, and Susan closed the door and went downstairs to the kitchen. She put together a tray with the wine, a glass and some cheese biscuits she had baked that afternoon. No one should drink on an empty stomach.

Monique held the door open for her and she placed the tray on the balcony table. 'You see, I've stopped shaking now,' said Monique, holding the glass that Susan had just poured. 'But there's only one glass. You won't join me?'

'Thank you. I will in a little while. I think I just heard a car on the driveway, so I'd better go and attend to whoever it is.'

Susan didn't normally drink during the afternoon but she felt Monique needed someone to talk to. She put the lamb she'd been preparing into the oven for slow cooking and then saw Eric coming in the front door.

'You're early,' she said as he passed the kitchen.

He stopped. 'One of my patients cancelled. I was hoping you had some more of that pinot noir we had last night.'

'Oh, I just opened it for Mademoiselle Debois. Sorry. She was a bit upset after her meeting today.'

'Ah, she must have been disappointed. She told me she was hoping to meet a relative, a nephew or cousin, I think.'

'No, it was worse than that, actually. She looked terrible. Ralph brought her back here and he said something about a shock.' She opened a cupboard and took out a wine glass. 'I promised I'd have a glass of wine with her. I think she's wanting someone to talk to.'

Eric smiled. 'I'll leave you to it then. Enjoy the wine.'

*

As he entered the dining room, Eric was looking forward to the roast lamb he'd smelled cooking all afternoon while he caught up on his case notes in his room. He was thinking about one of his patients who was much improved, and wondered if he had really done anything to help, or if the passage of time had done the healing. After all, Susan had done a similar job this afternoon just by listening to someone who wanted to talk.

'Do you mind if I join you?' Monique asked, approaching his table and holding a half-empty bottle of pinot noir. 'I need some help to drink this wine. And my mother always told me I should never drink alone.'

'Ah, that's very true, and I see you have a nice bottle there.'

'Now it's my turn to have a little joke on you,' Monique said. 'Susan told me it was your favourite wine and that this was the last bottle. So you're welcome to have it.'

'I would love some. Please have a seat, and I'll get the glasses.' Eric poked his head in the kitchen door' where Susan was carving the meat. 'Can I get two glasses please, Susan? They're in the cupboard here, aren't they?' He helped himself. 'Monique's joining me at my table. I think she's been crying. Is she all right?'

'She's okay. I offered to serve her dinner in her room, but I'm glad she's come down.'

After he'd poured the wine, he asked Monique about her meeting in town with Ralph. He expected the question might upset her.

'Ralph is a good boy, and he is my nephew, but he's not much interested in family. He has a lot of anger in his heart.' She sipped her wine and changed the subject. 'Did you do some more painting today?'

'I'm afraid not. Do you like this wine? We make good wine in Australia.'

'It's stronger than the wine in Brantome, very good, but I'm afraid if I have too much I'll get drunk.'

Susan served their meals and they ate in silence for a few minutes, broken eventually by Eric.

'You must be very disappointed to have come all this way…'

'*Non*, not at all.'

'What will you do now?'

'I don't know. I need some time to think. It's nice here, and Susan is a good hostess, don't you think?'

He didn't want to push her, so he concentrated on finishing his lamb. When she put her knife and fork down on a half-eaten meal, he broke the silence again. 'I'm hoping to finish my painting of the willow tomorrow morning…' He looked up at the painting on the wall. 'Do you still have that feeling of *déjà vu*?'

She followed his gaze. 'No, it's very strange, but that feeling has gone now, because now I remember. I remember what happened under the willow tree in Brantome, and I know this must sound mad, but I even remember forgetting. I remember telling myself to forget this ever happened…'

'Is this to do with your brother?'

'*Oui.*'

'How old were you?'

'Ten.'

'And what did he do to you?'

*

Monique studied the stranger opposite her at this table in a small hotel in Australia, so far from Brantome, who seemed to know her deepest secret, something so terrible she had hidden it from herself for over fifty years.

'I think you know what he did to me.'

Eric nodded. 'I've heard it before, many times. We call it repressed memory. When something happens that is so terrible you can't think about it, you try and forget it but it surfaces in dreams, nightmares.'

'And *déjà vu?*'

He nodded.

'My mother told me I must never tell anyone what happened. Jacques left home. He was eighteen, and I don't know if anyone knew where he went. But it turns out he came to Australia, where he had a child, Ralph, my nephew. And changed his name to Jack. Jack Woods. My brother spent a lot of time in prison.'

'I can understand why you're so upset.'

'It is a shock. I think I'm so stupid because I'd forgotten it. And Ralph is angry about his father because of what he did to his sister.' She wiped tears away with her serviette, then saw the smear of mascara on the white linen. 'Oh, I'm so sorry. I thought I'd finished crying.'

'Don't be sorry. It's normal to cry and it's normal to feel angry.'

'So I'm not mad?' She laughed through her tears.

'Of course not.' He seemed lost in thought, drumming his fingers on the table, then he stopped. 'In fact, I might be able to help. Do you know if your nephew's sister – she'd be your niece, wouldn't she – do you know if they live near Kyogle?'

'Yes, I think so.'

'Well, I think I know her, and I think she'd like to meet you.'

'Is she a patient?'

'I can't tell you that. I'll speak to her, tell her about you, if that's okay.'

'Of course.'

*

Dear Jane,

My friend Eric has lent me his computer and I am typing this email by myself. You can reply to this email address if you like. I just have to remember my password.

I have met some wonderful people and made friends here in Kyogle in just a few days. Tonight I am going to have dinner with my niece, her husband and their three children on their farm. The children are excited to meet a great aunt and I am excited to have a family.

I have also met my nephew, who sent the letter I showed you. Ralph is a nice boy but has not married and has no children.

I am glad I made this journey. It has been a big adventure. I might stay in Australia a little longer. My friend Eric is an artist. He does watercolours and nudes. He says I have a good bone structure. Do you think I should pose for him?

I hope you and your family are well.

Your dear friend, Monique.

The Fog

I stop at the front fence. There's fog, and I can't even see the houses on the other side of the road. If I go back inside, I can get my fairy wings. But I just remembered that they're at home and I'm at Granny and Poppa's house.

Everything's crazy. Where's Mummy?

Granny and Poppa aren't awake yet. Yesterday, Granny picked me up from kindy like she sometimes does, but Mummy didn't come to take me home. Last night I had to wear one of Granny's old shirts instead of my nightie and it's dragging on the footpath and getting wet. It's slipping off my shoulders, and I have to keep pulling it up.

I've got Mummy's handbag over my shoulder. The zipper doesn't do up, but that doesn't matter. It smells like her. I always play with it at Granny's. I can go shopping with my money that I cut out of paper with Granny's scissors, and Poppa's coins he gave me from his toolbox. They're shiny and golden and he makes them in his shed. There's something else in the bag. It's Mummy's wedding ring. It's a secret. I put it on my thumb but it keeps slipping off, so I put it back in the bag. When she comes to pick me up, she can have it again.

I feel like I might cry but I'm going to be brave.

Everything's different. I hate the fog. It's dirty and wet. Poppa told me I shouldn't be scared of the fog because it's just water but it doesn't look like the water that comes out of a tap which is clear and clean like glass, or the water in the pond which is shiny like a mirror, or the water at the beach which is bumpy and dark with soapy suds.

I've got my magic wand in Mummy's bag too. I try waving it around. I say, 'Fog, fog, go away,' but it doesn't work. So I sing the alphabet song, stepping out onto the footpath with each letter, which makes me feel a bit better except when I get to M and N, I have to stop because I've forgotten the rest.

There's no noise at all, except for a thump thump in my chest, and I can hear the air going through my nose as I'm breathing. I hold my breath and close my eyes. When I open them, the fog is still there.

I'm at the corner now and I can see the shape of the street sign over the road. It says Azalea Avenue and Granny's house is at number 14. I know that off by heart. Granny made me say it over and over so I wouldn't forget. She said it's easy to remember because there are lots of azaleas hanging over everyone's fences. They're light pink and white and a very dark pink, but they're all wet now and soggy and most have fallen onto the footpath and they're slimy and slippery if you tread on them.

I have to make the L sign with my thumb and fingers to remember which is left, because I've got to look to the left and look to the right before I cross the road. We sing that song at kindy.

There's too much fog. I can't cross the road because there might be a car coming.

I'm looking for Mummy. She's been swallowed up by the fog.

*

I remember being in the car when I woke up. Mummy and Daddy were shouting at each other. Then Daddy stopped the car and Mummy got out and I saw her disappear in the foggy dark. Daddy kept driving, down a hill, and he wouldn't stop and he wouldn't go back. I screamed and screamed, but he wouldn't.

We went all the way home without her. She was still there, somewhere in the fog. She'll be lost. It was a big hill. With trees all around. There weren't any houses. I wet my pants. When we got home, he said for me to go to bed. He was scary, with eyes like the big bad wolf, so I took my clothes off and got into my nightie all by myself and I stayed in my room. I was listening for Mummy to come home. When I closed my eyes, I thought she was there. I crossed my fingers and made a wish for her to be there, and I wasn't going to open my eyes until I knew she was sitting on the edge of my bed and I could feel her hand on my forehead, like always. But then I did open my eyes and it was still dark and I remembered the fog – but I thought it might have been a dream and she might be home after all. So I tiptoed down the hall and looked through the crack in the door of the lounge room where the light was on, and it was just Daddy sitting there with those scary eyes. He saw me and it looked like he got a fright because he spilled some of his drink on his trousers.

'Go back to bed,' he said.

'But I want Mummy.'

'She's not here.'

'Can you go back and get her?' I came into the room.

'No. Now get back to bed.'

'But I want Mummy.'

He stood up and he was right over the top of me. 'Get…' he shouted, 'back…' he pointed to the door, '…to bed.' He growled like Richie's dog used to, and picked me up, and put me down again in the hall where it was dark. 'Now!'

*

'There you are.' It's Granny. She picks me up even though she's not supposed to because she's got a bad back. She hugs me so tightly she squashes all the air out of me, and her face is all wet. 'Don't do that again, Lily. You'll give me a heart attack.'

'I'm going to find Mummy.' I push against her and she has to put me down again because I'm too big now. I'm nearly five.

'Come with me, now,' she says, grabbing my hand and holding it tight. 'I've got a surprise for you for breakfast.'

'I don't want any breakfast.'

'Come on, Lily. Be a good girl and Poppa will make us some pancakes.'

'With maple syrup?'

'Yes, with maple syrup.'

*

I have to stay with Poppa while Granny goes to get me some clothes. I'm wearing another shirt of hers which is clean and dry, and my kindy clothes from yesterday are too dirty.

While she's gone, the phone rings and I think it might be Mummy so I run to get it before Poppa does. There's a man who asks me if my name is Lily and then he says he wants to speak to my grandfather.

Poppa takes the phone from me. He doesn't say much, just stands there nodding and saying 'Yes' and 'No' and then he sits down with the phone next to his ear, and he puts his arm around me and pulls me close to him so he can give me a cuddle.

He looks so sad when he hangs up the phone and I tell him I love him. I can see there's tears running down the cracks in his face. I sit on his knee and he strokes my head and I lean on his shoulder. We're still sitting like that when Granny comes back.

She's got new clothes for me. I thought she was going to get them from home, but she got them from a shop. There's underpants and a singlet and socks and a T-shirt with words on it, and a purple skirt. And a new nightie with flowers on it. I have to put them on to see if they fit. They've got labels on them which we have to cut off with the scissors I used to make my money. I tell her I can do it because I'm nearly five and she gives me the scissors, and watches while I snip off the labels and she pulls out the scratchy plastic thread.

'The police rang,' Poppa says.

Granny pulls him into the kitchen, so I can't hear what they're saying. But I can. I hide behind the door and listen. I'm good at hiding.

'They've taken him in for questioning…' Poppa says. I don't know what that means. 'They want to speak to Lily.'

Granny says some things about Mummy, whose real name is Gwyneth. Granny called her that when she was a little baby, because Granny is Mummy's mummy. And Poppa's her daddy.

'They've taken her to the morgue,' says Poppa, and Granny makes a funny sort of noise.

I feel happy again now they know where Mummy is, and I forget that I'm supposed to be hiding and I open the door into the kitchen. 'Well, what are we waiting for?' I say, putting Mummy's bag on my shoulder and my hands on my hips like she does when she wants Daddy and me to hurry up. 'Let's go and get Mummy from the mall.'

*

I'm sitting on the lounge between Granny and Poppa and there's a pretty lady sitting on Poppa's favourite chair and a man is standing behind it. They said they were police officers but I don't think so, because they're not wearing uniforms. There is one wearing a uniform. She's a girl policeman and she's making a cup of tea for everyone. That's not right either, because no one even wanted a cup of tea.

'My name's Katie,' says the lady, 'and you're Lily. This is Peter.' She looks up at the man behind her. 'And we're going to record what you say on this.' She puts the recorder on the table. 'Is that okay with you two?' she asks Granny and Poppa.

Granny nods, and Poppa says, 'I suppose so.'

So she clicks a switch and a little green light goes on. She's got long fingernails with red nail polish and a sparkly ring on her finger.

Peter speaks to Granny and Poppa. 'Has she said anything?'

Granny answers. 'She hasn't said much at all, but she's quite distressed. She gave us a bit of a fright this morning.'

'What happened?' asks Katie.

'She took off. Got it into her head that she was going to find Gwyneth. We found her up the road a bit.'

'My mother's real name is Gwyneth,' I tell Katie.

Katie nods and smiles. 'Now, Lily, I want you to tell me what happened yesterday.'

I don't know what she wants me to say, so I look up at Granny.

'Before I picked you up from kindy,' Granny says.

'I was at kindy,' I say. I'm trying to sit very still.

'Was she at kindy all day?' asks Katie, but not to me, to Granny.

'As far as we know,' Poppa answered. 'We always pick her up on a Wednesday afternoon, and we just assumed everything was normal.'

'Of course. Who took you to kindy, Lily?' asks Katie.

'Daddy did. Mummy wasn't home yet.'

'Where was your mother?'

'In the fog.'

'So, she wasn't home when you went to kindy?'

I shake my head, because I'm remembering telling Daddy that I didn't want to go to kindy. 'Daddy said I had to go to kindy and Mummy would be home later.'

'Did Daddy give you breakfast before you went to kindy?'

I nod. It was a slice of toast and a cup of orange juice. 'I got dressed by myself. I'm nearly five.'

'Are you going to big school soon?' she asks.

'Yes, but Mummy has to buy me a uniform first and new shoes.'

No one says anything for a little while.

'Granny said we can't get Mummy. Is Daddy going to get her from the morgue?' Granny said it wasn't the mall, it was the morgue, but I don't know where that is.

'Yes, I think that's probably where he is,' says Katie.

I can tell she's lying because of the way she looks at Peter. Maybe the morgue is a long way away, like when we had to get on an aeroplane once to go on a holiday, and there was a pool and a beach there.

'When is Mummy coming to take me home?' I ask.

No one answers. Granny puts her arm around me and my knees start shaking. I put my hands on them to make them stop. Inside my tummy it hurts and I might vomit.

'Who's your best friend at kindy?' Katie asks me.

That's easy. 'Rachel. She's five.'

'And you'll be five soon too,' says Katie. 'Is Rachel going to big school too?'

I nod. 'We'll be like sisters.'

She smiles and twists the ring on her finger.

'Is that a diamond?' I ask.

'Yes.'

'Did your boyfriend give it to you?'

'Yes.' She smiles with her whole face and I know she's telling the truth.

'Is Peter your boyfriend?'

'No.'

They both laugh.

'Are you going to get married soon?'

'Yes.'

'Can I come to your wedding?'

She looks a bit funny then, so I tell her about my auntie's wedding and how I was the flower girl, and she asks me what I wore and what my aunty wore and for a little while it's really nice and I don't feel sick any more and my knees are still.

Then she asks me about the fog.

I don't understand about the fog. It swallowed Mummy. She disappeared and went to the morgue, wherever that is.

*

I'm having a ride in the police car. It's blue and white and it's got a siren and lights on the top but the girl policeman who is driving it won't turn them on. She says they're only for emergencies. I wanted to sit in the front, but I'm not allowed. I'm in between Granny and Poppa, with Mummy's handbag on my knee.

The fog has gone and it looks just like a normal day.

We're going to the morgue.

Katie and Peter are in an ordinary car and they're driving to the morgue too. They said they'd meet us there.

We went to the morgue but I didn't see Mummy there. It was just a boring room, like at the doctor's with seats and magazines for people to read, and we had to sit down and wait for a while and then Katie sat down with me while Peter took Granny and Poppa away. I was a bit scared, like when I know I'm going to get a needle. I cried a bit until Katie found a book and she read the story to me. It was Cinderella. Then Granny and Poppa came back and we went in the police car again.

Now we're at the police station and we're going to see Daddy, but first we have to wait a while and there's another Cinderella book, which Granny reads to me, but I'm not listening because people are walking through the room all the time and each time I think it might be Mummy or Daddy coming.

Something's wrong with Daddy. His eyes are red and his face is wet. He gives me a hug then lets go and kneels down in front of me. 'For God's sake, Lily, tell them.' Then he looks up at Granny and Poppa. 'I didn't do it. You've got to believe me.'

'Where's Mummy?' I ask him.

Then he looks at me like he's only just noticed I'm there. 'Oh darling.' He wraps me in his arms like he used to do. 'Hasn't anyone told you?'

'She's too young to understand,' says Granny. 'We didn't know how to tell her…'

'Lily, darling.' Daddy picks me up and sits me on the table.

There's not much in this room. No windows. Just a table and two chairs and everyone is standing, except me. I'm sitting on the table and everyone is looking at me. That's Granny, Poppa, Katie, Peter. And Daddy.

He holds both my hands. 'Mummy isn't coming home again, Lily. She's gone.'

'Why?' Everything's going crazy again. I can't understand why she wants to stay at the morgue. If she comes home, I can give her ring back.

'She can't come home, Lily,' says Daddy.

'She's with God now,' says Granny.

'But she will come home soon, won't she?' I ask.

No one answers.

Instead, Granny says, 'I told you she was too young.'

'I am not too young,' I say. 'I'm nearly five.'

*

We're all sitting around the table now, except Daddy, who had to go out of the room. They've brought in some more chairs, and Katie wants me to tell her about the fog.

She says, 'You were in the car…'

'We were in the car,' I say. 'And I was asleep. Then Daddy stopped the car and Mummy got out.'

'Did you wake up and see your mother get out of the car?' Katie asks.

'Yes.'

'Why do you think she got out of the car?'

'I don't know.' I start crying and this time I can't stop.

Granny tries to pick me up but I kick and punch her till she puts me down again. Then Daddy comes into the room and picks me up and walks around the room with me in his arms, until it's just hiccups. All the time he's telling me that I'm being very brave and he's so proud of me and that I should just tell the lady what happened.

Someone's brought in an orange drink in a plastic glass with a straw. I'm thirsty and everyone watches while I drink it.

When they make Daddy go out of the room again, I scream and scream until he comes back. He's standing behind me, and his hand is on my head.

'Lily, I know this is hard, but it's very important,' says Katie. 'Can you remember anything about where you were when your mother got out of the car?'

'It was dark. There was fog.'

'Were there houses, street lights?'

'I couldn't see anything. I saw her disappear.'

'Why? What did your father do after she got out of the car?' asked Katie.

'He…' I look up at Daddy.

He nods. 'It's okay, Lily. Tell her.'

'Don't look at your father, Lily, please. Look at me,' says Katie.

'He wouldn't stop. He wouldn't go back and get her and she disappeared.'

'Before she got out of the car,' Katie asks, 'did your mother say anything or do anything that was strange or unusual?"

'I don't know. They were shouting at each other.'

'Were they having a fight?'

'I suppose so.'

'Do your mother and father often fight like that?'

I shrugged. 'I don't know. Sometimes.' I don't want to look at her any more. I wrap the straw from my drink around my finger, round and round, like a ring. I make it tight and my fingertip goes red.

Granny reaches over and takes it off.

'Do you remember what they were saying to each other?' asks Katie. 'Even if they're words you don't understand…'

'I know the words, but I'm not allowed to say them.'

'Well, you're allowed to say them now.'

'Mummy said the bad word. The really bad word. She told Daddy to fuck off.' I look down at my feet which are swinging under the chair, backwards and forwards, backwards and forwards. I think she might hit me, like Mummy did when I said that once to Richie who lives next door. He's only three and he was bugging me.

'Grown-ups sometimes say bad words to each other,' says Katie.

'It's okay, no one's going to be cross with you. Did she say that before she got out of the car?'

'Yes. And then Daddy stopped the car and she got out.'

I look up at her face and she looks kind. She's smiling at me and twirling her ring around on her finger again. Round and round, round and round. Mummy had a ring on her finger and it was really tight. She had to tug it to get it off. That's what she did when she got out of the car. She threw it at Daddy, through the window. It missed him. He didn't even see it, and I couldn't see it either in the dark.

'So what happened after you got home?' asks Katie.

'I went to bed.'

'Did Daddy come and tuck you in? Read you a story?'

'No.'

'Do you know what Daddy did after you went to bed?'

'No.'

'You didn't hear the TV go on?'

'No, he wasn't watching TV.'

'Did he go to bed?'

'No. He was in the lounge room. He was just sitting in the chair.'

'How do you know that?'

'I could see the light under the door, and then I got up and I saw him.'

'And what did you see him doing?'

'Nothing.'

'She's telling the truth,' says Daddy. 'I didn't go out. I drank half a bottle of whisky and passed out on the chair. That's where I was when she woke me in the morning.'

'Is that true?' asks Katie. 'Did you find Daddy asleep in the lounge room?'

I nod.

*

Daddy has to stay at the police station and they won't let him drive our car home, so I go home with Granny and Poppa in the police car again.

I close my eyes because they're sore from all the crying and I lean against Granny. Mummy's bag is on her knee and I can smell it. It makes me think I'm leaning against Mummy.

'Is she asleep?' Poppa asks, and I pretend I am.

'I think so.'

'Poor kid must be exhausted,' says Poppa.

'I don't know what to believe, do you?' asks Granny. 'I can't believe Dave would do something like that. And I just can't bear to think of her dying like that. Beside the road.'

I can tell Granny is crying because her voice goes up high and her chest is all twitchy.

'Shh. You'll wake Lily.'

I keep my eyes closed.

'What are we going to do with her if they decide to charge Dave?' asks Granny.

'They won't. It's got to be a hit and run.'

*

Poppa carries me in to bed and Granny dresses me in my new nightie. I'm finding it hard to stay awake, and I put my head on the pillow and then I remember Mummy's bag. I think it's in the police car.

I sit up suddenly. 'The bag, Granny. Where's Mummy's bag?'

'It's okay, darling. It's just here,' and she has it over her arm, after all.

She leaves it on the bed for me, and I wrap my arms around it and give it a cuddle, like the teddy bear I had when I was little. When they're out of the room, I reach into the bag and put Mummy's ring on my thumb. It was on the back seat of the car when Daddy took me to kindy yesterday and I picked it up and put it in my bag. I didn't tell Daddy because I thought I might get in trouble. I was going to give it to Mummy when she came to pick me up, but she didn't. Mummy says you mustn't just take things. That's stealing and the policeman will put you in prison if you steal things. So now I have to keep it a secret for a hundred years. A hundred is a lot. I can count up to twenty. One, two, three, four, five – I'm nearly five, six, seven…

*

'Where did you get that?' Granny has seen Mummy's ring on my thumb, and I'm in big trouble. I went to sleep with it still on my thumb.

Poppa's in the room now and he wants to know too.

She's taken the ring off my thumb and I have to go to the toilet. When I come back, Granny has her hands on her hips and she looks really angry. 'Did Mummy give it to you?' she asks.

I shake my head. 'Mummy threw it away and I picked it up.'

'When? When did she do that?' asks Granny.

'When she got out of the car. She threw it at Daddy but Daddy didn't see it.'

'Are you telling us the truth, Lily?' asks Poppa.

'Yes.'

'Well, I think we ought to tell Katie, don't you?' says Granny.

'No, you can't! Granny, please don't. I'll have to go to prison for a hundred years.'

But Poppa was already on the phone. It was too late.

*

Katie and Peter bring Daddy with them and he gives me a cuddle as soon as he sees me. He looks a bit better than he did yesterday.

I tell Katie and Peter the truth about the ring and she promises that no one is going to take me to prison. She says that she believes Daddy now. Daddy gives me the ring and I put it on my thumb. One day, my fingers will be big enough to wear it properly.

I go home with Daddy. Mummy still isn't there. He makes Vegemite sandwiches for us.

I still don't know where Mummy is.

'She's in the morgue for the moment,' he says. 'But it's just her body that's in the morgue. That's where Granny and Poppa went with you.'

'But I didn't see Mummy there.'

'No, they wouldn't let you see her.'

'That's not fair. I want to see her.' I throw my sandwich on the floor and he bends down and picks it up without even yelling at me.

'You're not old enough to understand some things,' he says. 'Mummy has been killed. She got run over.'

'Like Richie's dog?' Richie's dog growled and barked at me when I came near the fence, so I was happy when it got run over and never came back.

'Yes. Like Richie's dog.' He takes a big bite of his sandwich. 'Sort of.'

'Was she squashed, like Richie's dog?' I ask.

'No. No!' He stands up, sits down again. Reaches across the table and holds my hand. 'Listen. The police – the lady and the man you spoke to yesterday…'

'Katie and Peter.'

'Yes, Katie and Peter thought I had run over Mummy.'

'But you didn't.'

'I told them that but they didn't believe me. That's why they had to ask you. They took the car to see if there were any dents on it. Anyway, they believe me now.'

'When can I see Mummy?'

'We'll have a funeral soon,' says Daddy, 'so you can say goodbye.'

'Will I see her?'

'No. She'll be in a coffin…'

'Why?'

'Because that's… Come on, eat your sandwich. You want to grow big and strong, don't you?'

'Why didn't you go back and get Mummy?'

'I don't know, darling. I wish I had. It was dark. I was angry. I'm sorry.'

He's crying and I give him a cuddle and tell him I love him. If people don't love each other, bad things happen.

We go outside and Daddy pushes me on the swing. I want to go higher and higher so my feet touch the sky, because the sun has sucked up all the fog.

Covers

After I'd finished for the day, I drove a few blocks from the surgery and pulled over in a quiet street, hoping none of my patients would see me. I tore open the envelope and pulled out the book. The cover was dark: a female figure with long skirts, carrying a candle, seemed to be hurrying down a hall, hair streaming behind her; there were shadows climbing the walls and in the doorways – vague, but I could see monsters and snarling mouths and teeth. The title, *In Darkness*, was written in red, like graffiti scrawled across a wall. In smaller print, *A collection of award-winning horror stories*. I thought it was a bit corny and looked like something I'd seen before.

I read my own story, and felt a jolt of pleasure, not only because it had been reproduced without error, but because I'd written it. Some people like making things with their hands, but this was something I had produced from my own imagination. It felt much more exciting than any of my more respectable achievements, such as studying medicine and becoming a general practitioner. It was my first published story, under a nom de plume of course. I couldn't tell anyone, or show anyone who knew me. What if they recognised themselves in my story?

I was itching to read the whole book from cover to cover, but time was short. I slid it into my voluminous handbag and drove home. I was the breadwinner of the family, and Peter was playing house-husband, looking after the twins while studying for his PhD. Amy and Eric would be waiting for me to read them a story before bedtime, and they liked stories with happy, uplifting endings and no monsters, please.

For as long as I could remember, I've had a secret life. It's not that I'm antisocial, I enjoy people, love my friends and family and care about my patients and their needs and fears. It's just that there seemed to be two of me: Sarah with an h, and Sara: one who lived in the real world and one who lived in a parallel universe. Sarah fulfilled all her responsibilities, smiled and laughed often, was an excellent wife, mother and daughter. Sara, though, was disobedient as a child, a reckless teenager and an adult short story writer. Sarah felt guilty for Sara's secret life.

At least, I told myself, I'd never acted out any of my wilder fantasies – well, almost never.

*

At one in the morning, Eric had asthma and came wheezing into our room. I took him back to his own bed, and helped him with his asthma puffer, and after a while he was breathing easily and his eyelids fluttered closed.

Instead of going back to bed, I fished the book out of my bag and settled in the lounge room to read it, starting with the first story. It had been written by a John Smith and had won first prize in the same competition I'd entered. I'd known a John Smith once, but with a name like it could be anyone, and was probably a nom de plume.

The story was called 'In Darkness' – the same as the book title.

The first paragraph was familiar. I read the second paragraph. My heart began to race. It was a story I'd written as a schoolgirl. I scanned the rest of the story; there might have been minor changes, but it was definitely my story – a story I'd handed in to my English teacher, Mr John Smith, in Year 11.

How dare you, Mr Smith! Goosebumps rose on my skin.

I closed the book, seeing the cover once again. Of course, that was why it was familiar. It illustrated this story – my story. It was my imagination, not his!

A shadow fell across me, and I almost jumped out of my chair. But it was only Peter, hair all messed up, standing bleary-eyed in the doorway.

'Are you all right?' he asked. 'I heard voices.'

Was I talking to myself? 'Yes, yes, I'm fine. Eric had some asthma, but he's okay now.' I tried to hide the book under my dressing gown.

'What's that you're reading?'

'Oh, nothing. Just a book one of my patients gave me. She's got a story in it.' Lying is so easy when I'm in Sara's skin.

Peter picked it up and studied the cover. 'Looks pretty gruesome. What sort of person writes this rubbish anyway?'

I shrugged and took a deep breath. I felt like crying.

'Come to bed, darling, you look exhausted.'

'I was feeling a bit restless, that's all.'

'Sounds like you need a massage.' He bent and kissed me, then helped me to my feet and led me into the bedroom.

*

The massage and the sex that followed were a pleasant distraction, but soon Peter was snoring beside me and I was wide awake again, remembering Mr John Smith.

In Year 11, all the girls were in love with him, and even then, no one quite believed that was his real name. He was a young teacher and a good-looking male in an all-girl school.

I was no better than my classmates. At night, I dreamed about him, wildly exotic and sexy dreams that belonged to Sara; not the schoolgirl who was diligently studying English literature, but the one who fantasised about orgasmic love scenes with Mr Smith.

My parents and teachers expected me to do well in the final year exams, and when not giving in to the my very private daydreams, I focused my English literature studies on American nineteenth century short story writers and poets, especially Edgar Allan Poe, who looked remarkably like an old-fashioned Mr Smith.

I incorporated Poe into my fantasies when I learned that he had married his cousin when she was only thirteen years of age and he was twenty-six.

I was sixteen when I wrote 'In Darkness', and heavily under the influence of Poe. Mr Smith would also have been in his mid-twenties. I handed the story in as my creative writing assignment in the last term of the year, and about a week later Mr Smith handed it back with an A+. He put a note on it that he thought my imagery was very interesting and, if I wanted to discuss it, he would be pleased to meet with me after school.

Of course I wanted him to help me with my imagery!

We met in a ground-floor classroom and he sat behind the teacher's desk in front of the blackboard, while I sat on a pupil's chair pulled up close to his desk. I could smell coffee on his breath as we leant over my story, and the wicked Sara imagined kissing him.

He underlined my words – *dark corridor, leading nowhere, shadows, growing like moss on the walls* – which was where my story's heroine was searching for someone, who by the end of the story she discovered was really herself.

'So, this dark corridor is an internal place?' said Mr Smith.

I nodded.

'It's somewhere inside Edith, your main character. It's a strong image, but I wonder if you really understand it.'

'I think so,' I said. I tapped my chest, between my breasts, and leant forward, wishing he could see my cleavage under my school uniform. 'It's inside me, a darkness.'

'Yes, you are this girl, Sarah, aren't you? Looking for yourself. This search for identity is quite normal in adolescence.'

I didn't like being called an adolescent, and was determined to prove I was much more mature.

'So, do you think this image is sexual?' I asked.

'Freud would probably think so,' he smiled. 'Women have dark secret places...'

I blushed. I had researched Freud, the psychoanalyst. I knew about his symbolism.

'You mean we have vaginas.' I couldn't believe I was talking to a schoolteacher about such things. It was like talking to my girlfriends.

He nodded, cleared his throat and read a bit further down the page, reading aloud and underlining: *her candle, flame flickering tentatively as she moved, the warm wax dripping onto her hand.*

Bad Sara had taken over by now and I saw the candle in my hand like a penis, the warm wax like semen. I laughed, feeling quite reckless. 'Freud would say that's a phallic image,' I said. 'Maybe a bad case of penis envy!' I was flirting, in a fairly obvious way, with Mr Smith and he wasn't objecting.

He laughed too. 'Yes, he certainly would.'

Did I make him blush?

And so we continued trawling through my story, examining the images, and I was wondering if he was getting turned on by me, until we reached the end of the story, when he stood slowly, picking up his briefcase as he did so and holding it in front of his body – to hide his erection, I was sure.

He held out his free hand and shook mine. 'Keep up the good work. Have you got a copy of the story on your computer?'

I nodded.

'Do you mind if I keep this?'

'No, by all means.' I said, and, tossing my hair away from my face in what I thought was a most seductive way, I left the room.

*

That wasn't the end of it. For a while, Sara overruled Sarah. I found it difficult to concentrate on any other subjects, and lived for my English literature classes. Of course I was discreet. I said nothing about any of this to anyone. I believed I was in love, and that secretly he was too. Given the right opportunity, Mr Smith and I were destined to become lovers.

It was nearly the end of the year when I wrote that letter to him – that awful, awful letter. I can't remember it word for word, and I hope he did the right thing and destroyed it. In the letter, I confessed my love for him, and told him that I knew he loved me too, and that we were like Edgar Allan Poe and his young wife Virginia, who was only thirteen when they married, and how her tragic death had inspired him to write all those wonderful stories and poems. I rambled on about the name Virginia and that she, like me, was a virgin, with *an untouched vagina* (an unfortunate phrase I remember only too well), and tried not to sound like an infatuated schoolgirl with a crush on her teacher.

He ignored me in the remaining classes that year. He literally looked the other way whenever he found himself glancing in my direction. I'd put up my hand to answer a question he'd asked the whole class and he completely avoided me. At the end of one class, I stayed back while he was packing his briefcase.

He just said, 'No, no,' before walking out of the room.

I ran after him down the corridor but he got away.

He didn't come back the next year, and I've often wondered if I ruined his teaching career.

I was heartbroken, until I reasoned that he was probably protecting me, waiting until I was older and despite knowing how illogical that kind of thinking was, I continued to use it in my fantasies. I turned him into a self-sacrificing hero. Then I met Peter at uni, and recovered my sanity.

Nothing ever happened with Mr Smith. I blamed it on Sara, the naughty one who as an adult writes secret stories.

*

Having drifted off at about five in the morning, I slept in until seven o'clock. Peter was already up getting breakfast for the twins when I emerged from the bathroom. He was at the kitchen bench with the anthology in his hands.

'Hi,' he said. 'Thought I'd let you sleep in because you had a bad night.' He put the book down to butter some toast for Eric, then picked it up again. 'You know, some of these stories aren't bad. That first story, the one that won, it's really good. Deserves the prize, I think. It's not the one your patient wrote, is it?'

I smiled. The good Sarah was in control again. 'No, she wrote the one called "Son of a Witch". She's Edith Anna Poe, which is not her real name. I think it's a homage to Edgar Allan Poe. I've read it, but I'd be interested to know what you think.'

He may or may not read it. It doesn't matter. His day will be just as busy as mine.

I couldn't think of any legitimate way to expose Mr John Smith's plagiarism without revealing my real name. To hell with him. He took advantage of a love-sick sixteen-year-old in more ways than one. A little blackmail might do the trick. I wondered if Sara, the horror-story writer, might write a threatening letter to Mr Smith.

Then Sarah urged Sara to wait, and that familiar tug-of-war between my two selves began fuelling my imagination for another story.

Shadows

There's someone over there, in the trees around the edge of the park. I saw his shadow and it moved.

Maybe it's Dad. If Dad came back, then he could take us to the park, he could play cricket with us. Mum tries, but the way she throws the ball is stupid. Girls can't throw. Still, gotta give her points for trying. That's what Dad says all the time about Josie. She's my sister and the only girl apart from Mum. I've got three brothers. Ben's the oldest – he's nearly twelve and he'll be going to high school next year; and Josie's ten; then there's me – I'm nine; and after me comes Daniel, who's seven. Max is the baby. He doesn't even go to school yet.

There's a peacock in the park. Mostly it hides from us kids, but it's out in the open today, where we play cricket. Maybe something scary is in the trees and it thinks it's safer in the open. It's pretty dark in the trees, but I've got a stick. I'm going to have a look.

When Dad left, Mum said, 'Good riddance,' but Miss Fielding at school said no one should ever say 'good riddance', because it's not a nice thing to say. I think Mum was angry. That's why she said it.

It's Sunday, so we don't have school today. On Sundays, we used to go to the park with Dad and we'd have a game of cricket and kick a football around. It used to be more fun with Dad.

'Rick? Rick? Come back here.' Mum's calling me because she can't see me in the shadows.

'I'm just here, Mum,' I say and I run back to them.

We have a tree we use for the wicket and Ben's got the bat. Josie's gonna bowl to him and she wants me to field, 'cos Daniel's gone walkabout again. He never pays attention. He's got the football under his arm and he's following the peacock around.

Last week the peacock spread out his tail for us and Mum said he's probably got a girlfriend and I thought she was talking about Dad. I know Dad's got a girlfriend because I saw him with her when I was down at the shops, and I was surprised when Mum said that, because it was a secret. Dad said I wasn't supposed to say…not to anyone. But Mum wasn't talking about Dad, she was talking about the peacock. That's what they do, peacocks, when they're trying to get a girlfriend. Like showing off.

It's very sunny and hot today and there isn't much shade, except in amongst the trees. My shadow, where I'm standing, is like a little puddle and my feet are in it. The sun is straight up above me. When it's time to go home, it will be lower and the shadows will crawl across the grass and it'll be hard to see the cricket ball.

Ben's hit the ball behind him, into the trees. That means he's out with our rules, because it takes too long to find the ball.

'I'll get it,' I say and I've picked up my stick and I'm bashing the plants and grass and then I see the shadow again and a blur of someone ducking behind one of the big trees.

It's a man. I'm sure of that. And I run after him, 'cos I'm sure now that it's Dad, but when I get to that tree he's gone.

'Rick, you found that ball yet?' It's Ben and he's calling me.

Mum and Josie have come into the trees now to help me look. They're looking in the wrong place. I can see it – a splash of red under a fallen log.

It's my turn to bowl and Josie's turn to bat. She misses and the ball bounces off the tree trunk, so she's out for a duck. She goes over to Mum and stands next to her. It'd be better if she stood further away but I'm not gonna say anything because now it's my turn to bat.

I'm standing near the tree trunk and it's Ben's turn to bowl. Max has gone over to Daniel, who is still following the peacock around, and he wants the football. They're gonna start fighting soon, but I've gotta watch the ball. It's a beauty. I slog it across the grass and everybody's running for it, so I manage to get four runs. There's no wicket at the other end, just a patch of ground that's a bit bare, and I have to touch it with the bat before turning around or it doesn't count.

Daniel's got a nosebleed and we have to stop playing so Mum can look after him. He's saying Max punched him and we all look at little Max. He's only three and a half and he's got the football under his arm and now he's following the peacock around.

Ben signals me to get ready to bat and he's tossing the cricket ball up in the air while we wait. So far I'm winning. I do some practice strokes like Dad taught me.

Then I see him. He's got his back to me, but I know that shirt. Dad has a shirt like that. My heart's beating real fast but I don't say anything, because he probably doesn't want Mum to know he's there. That's why he's hiding.

So, when everyone's ready to play again, I hit a high ball in Josie's direction and she catches it and looks at me like I'm real stupid. That means it's her turn to bat again, but first we have to give little Max a go and we all get in real close and Mum throws him a soft little ball and he hits it – *pow* – and then he runs and we all cheer him and he's real pleased with himself. Wants to have another go, so this time Ben bowls it to him and he misses it and I catch it and I tell him it's Josie's turn. Max is about to throw a tantrum but then he sees the peacock and takes off after it. I can feel Dad watching us while we're playing and think he must be feeling kinda sad.

Josie manages to score ten runs before she gets out after hitting the ball into the trees. I go after it again with my stick, and I'm on the lookout for Dad, but I can't see him.

Then I hear Mum calling little Max.

I find the ball and come out into the sunshine and there's the peacock, walking along the edge of the green where the shadows are spotty because of the leaves moving around on the trees, and it's pecking at the ground. Max isn't there.

Everyone's calling for Max and we spread out under the trees looking for him.

'Maybe he's hiding,' Ben says.

Max likes to play hide and seek but he usually chooses really stupid places and if you don't find him after a couple of minutes he gets bored with waiting and comes out from his hiding place.

'Maybe he's climbed a tree,' Josie says.

Only he isn't up any trees or under any logs.

And I'm getting really confused, because I saw Dad and I know Mum's going to go ape when I tell her. After everyone's given up looking for Max, I say that I saw Dad in the shadows under the trees.

*

We all have to go to school because it's Monday, and Dad's been on the news but no one knows it's our Dad because they didn't say our name. He's helping the police with their enquiries, and we saw him being taken into the police station with a towel around his head. They think he took Max because I told everyone I saw my father in the shadows, but I didn't really see him – not all of him. Lots of men have blue shirts and it's real dark under the trees. I might have got it wrong. I was wishing and wishing and wishing it would be Dad and that he'd come out of the shadows and he and Mum would kiss and make up and everything would be back to normal. And we'd finish our game of cricket with Dad, and Mum would play with little Max and he wouldn't get lost.

I tell Miss Fielding that I feel sick and I want to go home. The headmistress rings my mother but she can't come and get me, so I have to go to the sick room and lie down on the bed in there. I feel better by lunchtime because I want to be with Ben and Josie and Daniel.

We walk home together after school and no one says anything. We're all hoping like crazy that Max is found by the time we get home. Instead there's a policeman with Mum in kitchen and when Josie asks if Max is found, Mum shakes her head and starts to cry.

That night on the news they show a picture of little Max and ask if anyone has any information to come forward.

Dad comes home. I know now that it wasn't Dad I saw in the shadows. That man was bigger and sort of bent over. I tell this to the policeman who is staying with us to answer the phone if it rings. They think someone might have kidnapped little Max and want us to pay money to get him back, so no one is allowed to use the phone, except the police. Dad puts his arms around Mum and she looks like she's real glad he's back. I know I sure am.

We have McDonalds again for dinner and go to bed. Mum says we should say our prayers, and even though I stopped believing in God when I was eight, I get down on my knees and pray with Daniel and Josie and Ben. Praying is a bit like wishing for things and I'm scared now to wish too hard. Like I wished Dad would come back and he did, but I didn't want it to be like this.

Daniel doesn't want to sleep by himself, so he comes into the big boys' room (that's Ben and me) and gets into bed with me. Even though brothers aren't supposed to cuddle up, we do.

In the night, the phone rings and we get up. We're all standing in the lounge room looking at the policeman who is speaking on the phone. Ben whispers in my ear that it's the kidnapper asking for money, but the policeman is smiling and when he puts the phone down he tells Mum and us kids that they've found Max.

'And caught the man who took him?' I ask.

'Seems like it,' he says. 'Got pulled over for arbeetee.'

I'm trying to work that out while we all wait in the living room and when the police come with Max we're so happy to see him, we're pushing and shoving each other to be first to give him a cuddle. And he's okay. He's not hurt or anything.

When Mum says it's time for us to go to bed again, she goes with Max and Daniel into their room and Dad comes into the room with Ben and me, and he sits on the edge of my bed. I like the smell of him.

'What's an arbeetee?' I ask.

'It's not a word. It's the letters RBT for random breath test,' says Dad. When I still look confused he explains. 'You know how the police can pull you over and make you breathe into a little tube to see if you have been drinking alcohol? Haven't you been in the car when we've been pulled over…'

I get it. 'And they saw Max?'

'Yes. Without a seat belt.'

'And they recognised him from the TV?'

'That's right. We were lucky.'

I don't think we're lucky at all, but I don't say anything. He leans over to give me a kiss goodnight then moves his bum over to Ben's bed so he can kiss him good night too. When Dad turns out the light, I'm a bit scared of the dark like I used to be when I was little. I'm thinking of a man sneaking around under the trees in the park. I'm thinking of shadows.

Survivors

'Lizzie, wait here,' I say to my ten-year-old daughter. Flies swarm around her face and she holds a cotton handkerchief to her nose. We're standing outside a stranger's bedroom door and inside I can hear the flies. 'I'll go in.'

I take a deep breath and turn the handle. There are two corpses on the bed, but I avoid looking at them, focusing instead on the bedside tables, where I find their car keys. I grab them and exit as quickly as I can, trying to shoo the flies back into the bedroom as I close the door behind me – but it's hopeless; they escape under the door. Insects are excellent survivors.

We find the car in the garage.

'Fingers crossed,' I say as I climb into the driver's seat and put the key into the ignition. The engine sputters and stalls. Battery's low. I've brought a spare, which is outside. I've been siphoning fuel from cars to keep a generator running so I can charge up spare car batteries as I need them.

We walk back down the hall then outside, where it is a lovely day in the fresh air. A good day for a drive.

'Dad, can I go check out the garden?' asks Lizzie.

'Good idea. See if they have any fruit trees that aren't rotten with fruit fly,' I suggest. 'I can manage this on my own. When I get it running, I'll beep the horn.'

I try to shield Lizzie from as much as possible. She's too young to understand. I find it tough, but I can't imagine her heartache, the pain and loss she must feel. How does a child cope after seeing all her friends and family die? I know how much I miss my wife, Maureen. I often think we would be better off dead.

It takes a little while to remove the old battery and put in the new one. I try the key again and this time the engine sputters to life. The fuel tank is almost full, so we can cover some distance today.

There's a manual winder for the garage door, and soon I have it open. I put the car into reverse and beep the horn as I back out.

Lizzie comes running with two oranges. She looks happy with her prize. When she settles into the passenger seat, she drops them into her bag and pulls out our map. It started as a rough crayon drawing of the neighbourhood with fruit trees and cars drawn next to houses we had visited. The area we've covered has grown and it's become more sophisticated; now it needs to be unfolded, like a proper road map.

'Wait, Dad.' She finds a pencil in her bag and colours the small rectangle this house occupies green and writes *car and oranges* beside it.

I love the way she crinkles her nose when she writes – just like her mother.

'Let's go back home, get some supplies and then go exploring.'

'Are we going to put your notes up at shopping centres?' she asks.

'Yep. We'll find a country town. Might get lucky.'

It's a big car, so I can pack plenty of water, extra fuel and a spare car battery into the back along with some food for ourselves. We don't usually need to take much food for these journeys, because when we find a shopping centre, there'll be a supermarket with plenty of canned goods.

The streets are empty. I honk the horn periodically as we drive just in case anyone can hear us. The only noise, though, when we stop, is faint buzzing of insects, wind in the trees perhaps, and our own breathing. There are no birds, dogs, cats, cattle, horses or humans, apart from us. However, if we survived, there must be others – somewhere.

While I drive, I give Lizzie a geography lesson so she can grow up knowing something about the world as it was; and she, in turn, can pass that knowledge down to her children – when we find more survivors. She likes going to the library and picking books off the shelves – old-fashioned hardcovers and paperbacks. Electronic books are useless now.

'Dad, are we like Adam and Eve in the Bible?' she asks.

'Not quite,' I say. 'You might be Eve, but I'm not Adam. We need to find you an Adam, so one day, when you're older and when your body is ready, you can have children.'

'I hope he's nice.'

'So do I!'

'I'm a bit scared he won't be nice.'

'Me too. I'm hoping we'll find a few Adams for you, so you can take your pick. We've got plenty of time. You're still young.'

'We might find some Eves too, and I can have a best friend.' She rummaged in her bag again and produced *The Secret Garden* by Frances Hodgson Burnett. I was pleased that she'd started reading it, as it had been her mother's favourite.

After reading a few pages, she put the book down. 'Do you remember when I was little and you used to read me fairy stories?'

'Yes.'

'I'd dream of meeting someone like Prince Charming, but now I know that's stupid. I like this book. Do you think I'm like Mary? Wouldn't it be really really good if I could meet a boy like Dickon. And one day, when we both grow up, we could get married and have children. I wouldn't be scared if it was a boy like Dickon.'

Of course, she has to have her fantasies, and I'm not going to spoil them. Tears threaten and my throat tightens as I remember my own boyhood, my mates, and how important they were. My little girl is lonely and we must keep searching.

*

After an hour of driving, we are on what used to be a freeway. There are potholes and rockfalls but I'm used to driving in these conditions. We take an off-ramp. After a few hundred metres, I honk the horn and we pull over.

We both get out to pee – I go one way, she goes another – and we both listen to the silence. A breeze rustles the leaves on a tree. Or is it running water?

'Do you feel like going for a walk?' I ask, after we've been standing by the car listening for a few minutes.

She nods. 'That way.' She points down a slight hill. 'It must be a creek or something.'

'You never know what we might find.'

I believe if we explore sources of food and water, one day we just might come across other survivors like us.

*

The water looks good. It isn't covered in an algal bloom like most of the waterways we've come across. I scoop up a sample for testing.

Then we hear it.

Lizzie jumps. 'What was that?' She looks terrified.

'It might be a frog. Shh!' I hold her hand and we both stand very still, until we hear it again.

'There it is,' she whispers. 'Under that clump of grass.'

We bend down and watch as it catches a fly with his quick tongue. Lizzie giggles. I doubt she's ever seen a frog before except in storybooks.

'What should we do, Dad?'

'We'll leave it alone.'

'D'you think it's a boy or girl frog?'

'I don't know.'

'Maybe I should kiss it and see if it turns into Prince Charming.'

We both laugh. She reaches out to touch it, but it hops away.

This little frog gives me hope. He (or she) has everything he needs: plenty of insects and water. It's the first living thing we've seen in over a year, apart from insects.

In a pond nearby, we find some tadpoles, and I scoop a few into one of my specimen jars – not too many, just in case I can't establish a safe environment for them at home.

I have some yellow tape that I wrap around the area. We'll return here, and it'll help us find this place again. I also attach a note to a tree.

Hello, fellow survivor. If you come here, please let us know. We are a father and daughter, genetically resistant to the superbug that has wiped out most of life on Earth. You must be similar. Please leave a note, as we'll return. If you are mobile, you'll find us at 10 Smith Street, Haberville, our home base. Don't disturb the frogs.

*

Ten kilometres on, we find a town with a small shopping centre. There are six rusting cars in the car park. Inside the centre, it's dark. We shine torches and call out. I begin my work of placing notes to fellow survivors on storefronts. We find a supermarket, a liquor shop and a furniture store with beds.

We'll camp overnight in the furniture store and I'll help myself to a bottle of wine and drink a toast to a little green frog.

That Night

The night Dad died, his snoring woke me. He was sleeping in my brother's room; Luke was away at cadet camp, and I assumed Mum had kicked Dad out of their bed because of the snoring.

I got up, tried to wake him, but without success, so I rolled him over, which stopped the snoring for a few seconds. By the time I'd reached the door, he'd started again, so I closed it and went back to bed. About three-thirty a.m., the snoring stopped.

That morning I slept in and was really annoyed because I would miss maths with Mr Moss in first period. I had a bit of a crush on Mr Moss and I got his attention by being good at maths. Not many girls liked maths. They all called him Mr Moss, but when he told me his first name – Roland – I nicknamed him Rolling, after a stone which gathers no moss.

Dad was brilliant at maths too and encouraged me because you needed good marks to get into engineering, which was what I was hoping to do after I finished school.

That morning, Mum was in the kitchen cooking breakfast – fried eggs and bacon. I ate it because it was unusual for her to be awake at that hour, let alone cook breakfast. Mum didn't go to work. She did a bit of bookkeeping for small businesses and was home most of the time. It meant she would start drinking early in the day.

That morning, Dad wasn't in the kitchen and I figured he'd either gone to work or he was still asleep. The door was closed to Luke's room, and I didn't give it another thought. I didn't even ask Mum where Dad was.

In the mornings, there were always empty grog bottles on the coffee table or in the kitchen. I hated the smell of it.

Then there was Uncle Joe. He wasn't my real uncle, of course, he was Dad's boss at work and the first time Dad bought him home to meet us he'd told us Joe was lonely, since his wife had died the year before, and maybe a home-cooked meal would do him some good. He didn't have any children. Well, we saw a lot of Uncle Joe after that – he became one of the family. Mum did the bookkeeping for his company and I know for sure he wasn't lonely, because Mum and Uncle Joe were lovers.

I know because one day Rolling gave me a lift home to pick up a maths problem Dad and I had worked on the night before. I'd meant to take it to school. So that day I was home early and after I'd opened the front door I passed my parents' bedroom, and saw Mum sitting up on the bed, naked, her back to me – I'm sure she didn't know I was there. I grabbed the notepad with the maths problem on it from my room and snuck out again.

'Is something wrong?' Rolling asked when I got back in the car.

'No,' I said, looking over my shoulder when I heard the front door slam. Uncle Joe walked down our path, doing up his belt, hair all messed up. I worked it out.

In the car, Rolling asked me to explain the reasoning behind the solution and I was finding it hard to concentrate, but then he prompted me and we got through it. He told me a bit about himself; that he played the clarinet. I didn't even know what a clarinet was, but I asked him if he could bring it to school one day.

When I went back inside, Mum was in her usual place in the kitchen, dressed and with a glass of wine in one hand and a cigarette in the other.

*

Just after lunch, the day Dad died, I was called away from class to see Miss Johnson, the headmistress. Everyone sniggered, because you usually got called to see Miss Johnson if you were in trouble for something, and I wondered what I'd done. Was it because I'd been seen with Rolling in his car? There was nothing wrong with that, even though he was young for a teacher and quite good-looking.

Uncle Joe was in Miss Johnson's office. The headmistress guided me to a chair, then left the room. Uncle Joe sat down, and I was thinking maybe there'd been a car accident, maybe Mum had been driving half-pissed, as she often was, and maybe she was hurt.

Uncle Joe sat opposite me and held my hand. 'I've got some terrible news,' he said. 'It's your father. He died this morning.'

What did he say? It took a moment to register.

Uncle Joe was waiting for me to say something. It was like I was looking at myself from outside my body, looking at myself sitting on this chair in the head's office, with Uncle Joe holding my hand, telling me that my father was dead.

'Are you all right?' he asked after a while.

I nodded.

'Your Mum's at home and Luke's on his way back from cadet camp,' he said as he helped me stand, his arm supporting my elbow.

I nodded, then my knees buckled as I tried to walk, and I sat down in the chair again. It was like the world had frozen. I couldn't understand what was happening. Miss Johnson was outside her office, on the veranda – I could see her through the window, talking to Mr Moss. One of the girls from my class came up to them and gave them my school bag.

I tried standing again and this time my knees locked into place and I walked out with Uncle Joe, walked past the headmistress and Mr Moss, out into the sunshine, down the street a little way to his car. He opened the door for me and after I sat in the passenger seat he did up my seat belt – like I was a small child. Miss Johnson followed and gave my school bag to Uncle Joe, who put it in the car.

'Why?' I asked, when he'd started driving.

'Why, what?'

'Why did Dad die?'

'Um, we don't know the cause yet. It might have been a heart attack, they think.'

'But Dad wouldn't have a heart attack...' I said. 'He's not old enough.'

'It can happen. Your mother found him this morning, after you'd gone to school. And he...' Uncle Joe didn't finish that sentence; he might have been going to say he was cold or he didn't wake up. 'Look, she's pretty upset. And I know you're upset too. Just be gentle with your mum, okay?'

We'd been having some rows, Mum and me.

When we got home, I went straight into Luke's room, but Dad wasn't there. There was some pink stuff on the sheet and pillow, which now I know was vomit, but that day it didn't make any sense to me.

'Where's Dad?' I cried, running into the living room where Mum and Uncle Joe were pouring themselves a glass of whisky.

'Darling,' Mum wrapped her arms around me, spilling the foul stuff on my uniform. 'He died. This morning. He's not here.'

'But where is he?' I meant, where had they taken the body?

'He's gone, darling,' she sobbed. 'Maybe he's in heaven.' Her lips trembled and she started sobbing and Uncle Joe put his arms around her.

I went into my room, slammed the door, flung myself on my bed and cried. 'Daddy, Daddy.' I felt like a little girl, like the time he took me to the Easter Show and I let go his hand and then I was lost, and all I could do was cry and call out for him.

*

Later that day, I heard Mum in Luke's room. When I went in, I saw she was taking the sheets off the bed and stuffing them into a garbage bag.

'I need to get this bed made,' she said, when she saw me. 'Luke will be home soon.'

'He's not going to sleep in that bed, is he?' I asked. 'Dad was in that bed last night. He was snoring and I couldn't wake him up.'

'You knew he was in here?' Mum asked.

I felt guilty somehow. Then she flung her arms around me again and we both cried until I pulled myself away from her.

'Dad died in this bed. Luke can't sleep there!' I said.

'Of course he can. It'll be all right. We won't tell him. Help me turn over the mattress, and we'll get some clean sheets…'

By the time Luke got home, his bed had been made and his room tidied and no one ever told him that Dad had died in his bed.

*

That was the worst day of my life so far, but after the nightmare was over, things actually improved. Mum stopped being a sad old drunk and sobered up.

An autopsy was needed before we could have a funeral for Dad, and I was told the cause of death was accidental overdose. Dad had consumed a lot of alcohol that night and then he'd taken some powerful sleeping tablets – which was why I couldn't wake him. He choked on his vomit like Elvis Presley.

After Dad's funeral, Mum told me that he was the only man in her life, and that Uncle Joe was a good friend but would never take his place. She may have wanted to tell me more, perhaps about her affair with Uncle Joe. Luke and I were also beginning to accept Uncle Joe in our lives, especially in that awful time after Dad's death.

Every day, Luke and I went to school and Mum would get dressed in good clothes and go to work for Uncle Joe, as his secretary. I was amazed at the transformation. If only she could have pulled herself together like this while Dad was still alive, it would have been so much better for everyone.

*

Luke and I left home, share-flatting with university friends. Uncle Joe helped with the university fees and Mum was okay, because she had Uncle Joe. They eventually got married.

Mum gave up smoking and put on weight and all those years of not looking after herself started to show on her face: bags under her eyes, a tight, pinched mouth, stained teeth. Uncle Joe found himself a younger woman.

Then Mum started drinking again and got sick – stomach cancer that spread to the liver. I moved back home to look after her. She became a full-on alcoholic, with whisky for breakfast, and most of the time she spoke rubbish. Mum cried a lot, mostly crying for Dad, and telling me she loved him, that no matter what, I had to know she loved him.

I managed to finish my engineering degree and Uncle Joe rang to congratulate me.

'You've got a job here, you know,' he said.

'Thanks,' I said, 'but I can't leave Mum. She's in a bad way.'

'Look, I hope you're not angry with me for leaving your mother.'

'No.' But I was.

'She loved your father, and he was a good man, a good friend.' He paused, and I didn't know what to say. 'I know what it's like to lose someone you love. When my first wife died, I was devastated, but there comes a time when you've got to look after yourself.'

'Well, I don't think there's much chance Mum will do that.' I said, trying to keep a lid on my anger.

'I wasn't talking about her, or myself. I'm worried about you, making a martyr of yourself, sacrificing your own life to look after your mother. Do you have a boyfriend?'

'No, I don't. Sorry about that. I should have by now, I know. Just haven't had the time.' I was so angry I slammed the phone down.

*

My days were busy with Mum. Bathing her, trying to get her to eat, to swallow her pills, with hopeless visits to doctors, who had all given up on her.

I thought about my life as a schoolgirl, when I was always ashamed of my parents and never had friends come home because I worried that Mum'd be drunk. Dad was bad too, but he started drinking later in the day, after work, and didn't get quite as drunk as Mum. I got so angry with them, especially with Mum. I told her she was disgusting. That was cruel, I suppose.

At least with Dad we had maths, and even when he'd had a few, he could still sit down with me and go through some problems. And, I guess, the fact that he managed to hold his job as an engineer meant the grog hadn't done too much damage to his brain.

Then I remembered Rolling, and I found him on Facebook. I asked him to be my Facebook friend and thought that was about the saddest, most desperate thing I'd ever done in my life. We started corresponding. He was still teaching and congratulated me on getting through engineering, but when he asked me where I was working, I told him I was looking after my mum.

For a few days, I revisited my childhood crush on Rolling. He didn't seem so much older than me now.

Then Mum died, which was a relief to everyone. Rolling came to her funeral with his wife, and he introduced me to her, told her I was his star pupil. I didn't have any other friends attend the funeral, because I didn't have any.

*

A few days later, I made an awful discovery.

The estate agent needed the original certificate of title for the property, which was going on the market. This caused me to search in cupboards and drawers I'd never opened before, such as the drawers in my father's roll-top desk. I found it in a folder along with the original marriage certificate for Mum and Dad, our birth certificates, and Dad's death certificate, probate, and so on. I pushed aside a wad of papers which were folded lengthwise with red tape around them, thinking I'd look at them later.

I poured myself a glass of wine and looked again at the papers now lying scattered on the floor of what used to be my father's study. That wad of paper was a coroner's report. There'd been an inquest into Dad's death (I knew that) and also a committal hearing (I didn't know that). My mother, had been accused of murdering my father. (Did I want to know that?)

Page one told me the result. After being charged with attempted murder, the judge decided my mother had no case to answer, so it never went to court or made the newspapers.

I rang Uncle Joe. 'What's this about a committal hearing? Mum, charged with murder?' I asked.

'Ah,' he said. 'I wondered if you knew about that.'

'Well?' I remembered that I'd been quite rude to him the last time we spoke. 'I'm sorry.' I found myself crying. 'It's just that I don't know what this is all about.'

'Your mother and I, we tried to protect you and Luke,' he explained. 'This detective, trying to make a name for himself, was determined to prove that your mother had poisoned your father, that night, the night he died. I'm sure you know your mother loved your father. His death was accidental.'

'Like Elvis Presley.'

'Yes, like Elvis Presley. He'd had a few too many, and drugs and alcohol don't mix.'

'But why? Dad wasn't stupid. He wouldn't do that.'

'Maybe because your mother had just told him about our affair.'

I went cold, remembering that night. 'I knew you were sleeping with Mum...'

'But your father didn't. It was a shock. Your mother told me he stormed out of the house and came back very drunk. She'd gone to bed, and he must have slept in Luke's bed...'

'After taking sleeping pills?'

'That's what the coroner's report says. They'd been prescribed for your mother.'

'He wouldn't be so stupid.'

'It was accidental. Accidents happen.'

That night. Earlier the night before Dad died, I'd been trying to study with Mum and Dad screaming at each other – and I hated both of them. Then quietness until the snoring started. I imagined Dad coming home, drunker than usual, going into the bathroom, taking the pills that had been prescribed for Mum – the pills Mum never took because of the warning to avoid alcohol. The coroner said Dad had taken quite a few of those pills.

'Are you all right?' asked Uncle Joe.

I remembered the calm after Dad's death, Mum looking so respectable each morning.

'Did Mum ever work for you as your secretary?' I asked.

'No, she did our bookkeeping.'

'So it was all a show, going to work each day when she was really going to court.'

'She did it for you,' he said. 'Her main concern was to protect you children from the…from the…'

'Truth?' I asked.

'It doesn't matter now.'

'But you and Mum…'

'We were both lonely, and your mother was fragile and vulnerable. I tried to save her from herself.'

I thought about that, then asked Uncle Joe, 'Do you think Dad might have taken that overdose on purpose?'

'I don't know. But I do know that your mother never stopped blaming herself for his death, even though she never actually gave him those pills. And I couldn't live with a woman who was so determined to punish herself for a crime she didn't commit.'

Before hanging up, he repeated the offer of a job, and this time I told him I'd think about it – and thanked him.